EMOTIONAL DEVIANTS

VIOLA TEMPEST

Emotional Deviants
© Copyright 2022 Viola Tempest

All rights reserved. No part of this publication may be reproduced, distributed, or transmitted in any form or by any means, including photocopying, recording, or other electronic or mechanical methods, without the prior written permission of the publisher, except in the case of brief quotations embodied in critical reviews and certain other non-commercial uses permitted by copyright law.

Any references to historical events, real people, or real places are used fictitiously. Names, characters, and places are products of the author's imagination.

Cover Design by CReya-tive

CONTENTS

EMOTIONAL DEVIANTS

VIOLA TEMPEST

PROLOGUE

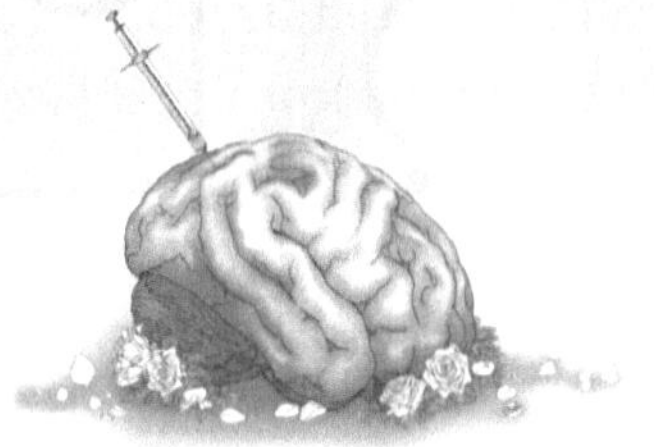

FAULKNER

The town of Bellevue was a desolate place. Not because there wasn't anyone around nor because the town was empty. No, the town was full of people: people who walked back and forth with their eyes glazed over, their expressions unreadable. It was desolated because it was empty of emotions.

Almost forty years had passed since Dr. Theodore

Faulkner became the supreme leader of the town. His name had been plastered all over the city, his discoveries and the invention of Siero changed the lives of everyone around him.

The scandal after the first trials, where a whole psychiatric hospital had been emptied of its patients that later committed suicide, had almost been forgotten by the population. No one cared about it, because there was no sense in feeling bad about it, about something that had happened so long ago. Actually, there was no sense in feeling: because there were no feelings.

Not at all.

When Siero had proved its worth, Faulkner himself had run for mayor of the town. His face had been over every single post and window, and people had praised him for his discoveries. Mental illnesses were a thing of the past, and his discovery had changed the lives of many.

When the time for the elections came, Faulkner won without a struggle. He rose to power, and slowly, from the inside, he started to change everything. Siero became mandatory in his first five years in power, and within a few years, there was not a single person left in Bellevue who hadn't had the shot.

The vaccine kept changing through the years, and as Faulkner got drunk on his power, the vaccine mutated. People went from having no mental illnesses to having no feelings whatsoever. Babies were given the shot at birth and were raised to become what society needed of them.

In the present, no one could feel a thing in this desolate bubble town.

———

Faulkner watched people walking past from his window on the tenth floor, his mind far away as he thought about anything else that might be needed for that night's event.

The throngs of people looked almost organized as workers headed home, and they formed lines to get onto the subway and buses. There were no arguments, no fighting over places in line, nothing. He still remembered how people used to get violent during this time of day, as if too eager to go home to keep being civil. He hated it.

Faulkner turned back to the desk and looked at the picture sitting there, slowly lowering to sit on his chair. The image was burned by the sun, but the happiness in his son's eyes was still unmistakable. He groaned as he sat, his joints making it hard to move, but he refused to use the cane unless he really needed to. So many years working on this, trying to make the best of this society, and now, the damned red reports filled his desk. He opened one, his shoulders sagging as he saw the statistics. More and more cases.

"I can't believe this is happening," he huffed.

More aberrations kept showing up, and his classified scientific team still hadn't figured out why, or how to stop it. Not many people knew about what was going on, and keeping the secret was getting harder and harder. Faulkner needed to get it over with, to cut the problem from the root, but he couldn't seem to find that root.

Some believed it was genetics. Others, faulty vaccines. He didn't care what the answer was, he just wanted results.

Almost ten years ago, he had managed to sell his vaccine outside of Bellevue. The version of the vaccine being shipped overseas wasn't the same one that he was using for his own town, no. He still needed an advantage, a reason for them to buy from him, and a way of making more money. The serum he had sent overseas was a milder version of the original vaccine, one that got rid of the mental health illnesses but allowed people to still feel. He needed wars so he could send his own heartless soldiers to fight those battles.

After all, the black market paid good money for his Blackhats, and he couldn't afford other places having an army as good as his own. The town's safety came first… but that didn't work if aberrations kept showing, and small riots kept taking place within the walls of Bellevue.

Annoyed and tired, he closed the files and headed toward the elevator. It was late, and he had to get ready for the party. The receptionist barely lifted her head to look at him as he passed, and didn't attempt to wish him a good night. She simply turned her head back down and kept working, as she was assigned to.

The Bluecoats' Annual Celebration was important for him and his reputation. After all, the Bluecoats were the ones who had his back, and someone from that tier would soon become the next leader, as Faulkner knew his days were numbered. He was getting old, and without any progeny of his own, he needed to pick a leader to replace him when the time came. He needed to find someone he could trust, someone who would make sure things kept getting better.

CHAPTER
ONE

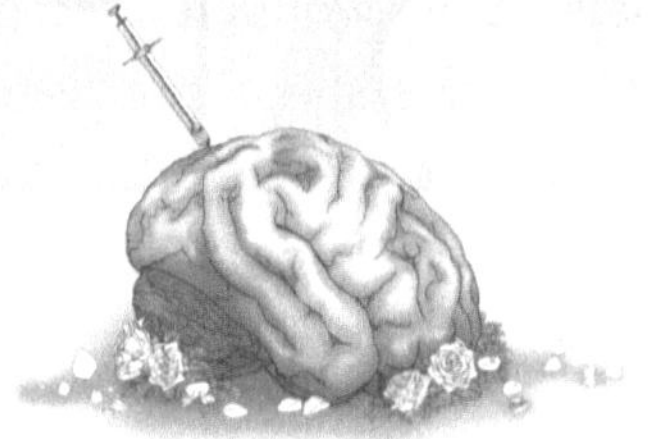

ANNA

The party looked the same as every other year, and Anna Chaplin lingered around the banquet table, munching on the tasteless food as she looked around the room. The venue was huge, decorated with big chandeliers and flower bouquets all over the place. It was the definition of wealth, and even if she wasn't from the lowest tier in society and had attended the ball for years, she still felt out of place.

"So lucky," a girl by her side said.

Anna raised a single eyebrow while looking at the teen by her side, who was grabbing a heap of chocolates and shoving them in her mouth, one by one.

"Who's lucky?" she asked, unable to contain her curiosity when the girl kept looking around the room, her eyes expressionless and bored.

"The Bluecoats and their vials. I sometimes wish I could see what it's like, you know…"

With a shrug and a noncommittal grunt, the girl walked away, her expression back to being blank.

For a moment, Anna wondered if the girl could feel anything at all, but she shook her head, disregarding that thought. Of course, she couldn't. She watched the group of Bluecoats close by instead, and caught one of the men, just as he was grabbing a small blue vial from his pocket and tipping it into his drink. It was the group the teen had been watching, and the men there looked just about her age, maybe a few years older.

Joy, Anna thought with a sad feeling in her gut.

She felt the emotion creeping onto her face, and she made sure to shift her expression back to its usual blankness before anyone could see her. It was a trick she had learned real young, but still, once in a while, she felt things surging toward the surface.

She knew everything about the Blue Joy vial. After all, she was an intern at the same lab where it was being produced — the Emotions Wing at the Fox Lab. Blue

Joy was a mixture of serotonin, dopamine, oxytocin, and even a touch of adrenaline. It was great for parties as it didn't have any adverse symptoms when consumed along with alcohol; it even heightened the effects of it.

The young girl from before was now lingering at the edges of the room, wandering with curious-looking eyes every time someone pulled a vial out from their pocket. Anna wondered if she was a Gray, but it couldn't be. Grays were never invited to Faulkner's parties, and that curiosity was surely something she was imagining. She wanted so hard to find feelings in anyone who wasn't a Bluecoat, that sometimes, her mind tricked her.

The party was mostly for Bluecoats — the businessmen and landowners of Bellevue — the ones who had been by Faulkner's side since the start and made sure to keep him in power. It was a celebration of everything they had managed so far, and a way for them to network and stay close together. They were a tight-knit group. This was why they were the only ones able to acquire the emotion vials — at least legally, as it was a way to reward them for all their hard work. They were also the ones with all the perks and almost none of the negative—

"Anna, darling. You shouldn't stare," her mother said as she showed up by her side, cutting her train of thought.

Glenn's shoulders were square, her chin held high. Her eyes blinked at regular intervals, her smile only showing when politically correct as she had been taught as a kid. The same teachings had come down to Anna when she was little, and she struggled to understand them at first. She had always been a smart kid, and it had only taken her a little while to notice that she was different. And only a little more to understand that *different* meant *dangerous* — that she had to blend in, to be invisible if she wanted to survive.

"I'm not. I was analyzing the composition of the Blue Joy vial in my mind, so I wasn't blinking because of the focus in my work," she lied with ease.

"Well, I admire your focus on your internship, but this is no place for formulas and work. You should go talk to some people. You know, ranking can get better if you connect with the right influences."

Anna nodded, "Of course, Mother."

Her mother barely looked at her as she walked away, her expression seeming almost bored. Whiteshirts weren't allowed to have emotion vials, so her mother had never experienced any kind of feeling. She knew almost everything about them from her work in the lab but had never experienced it for herself.

Same with her father. Frederik Chaplin, same as Glenn, was part of the administrative staff in one of the government bio labs that made drugs and serums, including the vials. This was the reason why Anna knew so much about the working of emotions, and why she had been granted the internship at the Fox Lab.

Having both of her parents working there had granted her easy access, and her future was almost set in stone. She'd work there her whole life, eventually be married off to some other Whiteshirt, and get some time off to have kids and keep the society working.

She hated it; she hated all of it. She knew she was lucky to have been born in the second most important tier of society, but still, she hated how her whole future had already been decided for her.

Tired of just watching and unable to disobey her mother's command, she decided to search for a group of people who looked high enough on emotions to be interesting. There was a group of girls about her age giggling, but that looked like too much — she might laugh at a joke and then have them figure out that she was only a Whiteshirt, which could get her in trouble.

Anna wasn't technically allowed to take emotion vials either, not even at a party like this. Looking around the room some more, she found a group of older gentlemen, about her parents' age, and made her way there.

"I can't believe the outrage of the situation between the Grays," a man was saying as she approached.

She tried to blend into the group, bobbing her head a little as the rest of the people did, and copying their postures as much as possible. She had been doing it for so long, that she wasn't even aware when she's copying the way other people moved or talked.

"I heard someone is smuggling out vials," another man whispered as if it were a secret.

Anna guessed it was, at least, among the commons. She couldn't believe her luck in overhearing such a conversation, so she perked up a little and listened in while saving each word the men said into her memory.

"I think Faulkner should put harder measurements in place to make sure this doesn't get out of control. Imagine all those Grays revolting because they're feeling too much. We could have the next Civil War coming our way."

"I think you're being dramatic, Mr. Tussels," the first man said.

"Not dramatic. There's no vial for that. I only took some enjoyment this evening."

A few people fake-laughed at the joke, and Anna bobbed her head a little.

"What about the fights? Did you hear about them? I heard they arrested a Gray last week who broke another man's nose. When they tested him, it looked like he had three vials of anger on him. I didn't even know those were still being stocked. I thought only positive emotions were being fabricated in the labs."

Anna bit her tongue so as not to get into the conversation. There was so much the Bluecoats were oblivious to. They might be the most powerful class, the ones with all the money, but they were also being manipulated by Faulkner without even realizing it. There was so much that was hidden from them, and Anna had only found out herself after lots of investigations.

Anger, betrayal, even fear… they were all used to enhance the reactions of the troops and make them more reactive. The Fox Lab had been running tests for months, while sending new troops outside of their borders, and Anna knew how they had gotten out.

"I think Faulkner is getting too old to know what

he's up to," someone said in a low whisper that was almost inaudible.

"Careful what you say," another retorted.

That comment alone could mean prison time if the wrong person had heard it, and the man knew it. He was too high on confidence and joy to be able to worry about the consequences of his words.

"Well, that's why he's looking for a replacement. I hear he's having some interviews at the moment, looking for the next in line to take leadership."

Not being able to handle it anymore, Anna slipped out of the party and made her way to the terrace of the building, where she found herself alone. Listening to all those conversations was just too much, and hiding her emotions got exhausting after long periods of exposure. It was one of the reasons why she enjoyed being an intern at the lab so much, as most of the time, she was on her own, hiding inside the lab.

The lights in the town were on, looking like tiny spots from high above. She could see the city center, with many of the tiny spots, and how the lights dimmed a little as she looked outwards.

The outer city was where most of the Grays lived, between the Capitol and the huge walls that surrounded the town. Her home was a little to the west, nestled in between the Capitol and the outskirts, just where most of the labs and government facilities were.

"What is it like out there?" she asked out loud, enjoying the loneliness of the terrace and the sound of her own voice.

She had wondered that many times, but could rarely

say any of it out loud. When she was younger, she had been naive enough to ask a few of those questions, and her mother had been terrified, explaining that she wasn't meant to ask any of those things.

Anna hadn't understood then, but soon, she did. She was different, and the things she felt deep in her gut were not normal. It was dangerous for her to voice any of it, and she didn't think she had done so since she turned six years old. It'd been hard to learn how to hide it all, every tear, every emotion, but her mother stopped worrying once she stopped showing signs of "illness," as Glenn had called it.

Working in the labs was the perfect way for her to find out more, to figure out why she was the only one in town who could… feel. It was scary most of the time, like she was walking among monsters that could tear her apart at any moment, but she had to keep going. She had to be invisible for as long as it might take until she had her answers.

Anna refused to play her part and simply survive. That was all she had done for years: being a survivor. Hiding in the shadows, pretending like pain and doubt didn't lace every step she took. Hiding the happiness she felt the first time she found an old record and listened to music, her eyes welling with tears that she quickly wiped away. She had hidden every emotion, every tiny thing she had ever felt, all to be one more in the crowd.

To be just another one of Faulkner's lifeless zombies.

But it was over. She wouldn't just survive anymore; she wanted to live. She'd find out the truth. She'd keep working in the lab and running her tests, figuring out how this all had come to be, and why there were still people who had feelings…

Even if she was the only one.

She refused to be a zombie.

CHAPTER
TWO

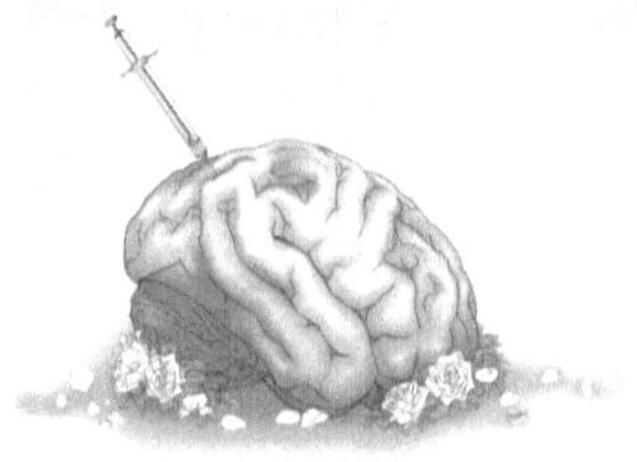

WINSTON

The town was oddly quiet in the late afternoon of that third Friday of the month. Winston had been stationed out there for a while now, and he had gotten used to the frequent brawls that he had to split up. There were more detentions in the past two months than there had been in years, and he wondered if something was stirring.

He was used to that particular Gray settlement by now, knew every street, every corner, and even some of the people were starting to look familiar after running into them over and over again. There was even a tavern in the south that he had gone to a few times with his pals on his days off, as it served some of the best beer that the town had to offer.

It wasn't that he wanted to feel familiar there. After all, it was a gray and sad place to be, but he sometimes felt more at home there than he did at his base. Maybe it was the memories of his mother and what she had told him, about what it was like to live there. Not that there had been any emotion to her tales, just simple facts, but ones that he had committed to memory.

"Mad Dog to Alfa One, do you copy?" His intercom beeped after the message, and he took it off of his belt, letting the memories slide to the back of his mind.

"Alfa One, copy," he said while pressing the button on the top.

He was walking down an empty street, the dim lights casting long shadows as he moved, and he looked around, making sure everything was in order. It had only been a few months since the Blackhats were deployed to the Grays' settlements, and it was unusual for them to send cadets to the field.

But since Winston was in his last year and close to graduating, they had made a few exceptions with his squad. They were treating it as some kind of advanced training, in which they could experience the work first hand — like an internship of sorts.

"There's a possible suspect of emotional abuse in the corner of fifth and fourth. I'm about to engage. Over."

"Copy that. Proceed with caution, Mad Dog."

He checked the map in his portable device and jogged toward the place of the disturbance. He wasn't too far away, and Mad Dog was sometimes stronger than he realized, so he'd just make sure everything was okay. Their shift would be over in half an hour anyway, so they could head back to the Military Academy together. He set his hand on top of his gun, just in case, and quickened his pace.

A little surge of adrenaline kicked in as he got closer to the corner and saw a man lying on the ground, but he shifted his expression to nothingness.

"Mad Dog, report," he said once he was at earshot.

John was handcuffing the suspect, a knee on his back, and sweat pearled his features.

"Suspect fought back and rejected his sentence. He's being taken to the lab to test his blood for anger levels. I injected him with a sedative."

"I'll go with you. Let me send a command to base."

He quickly got his screen out and typed a message. The night had been pretty chill, so he was sure leaving a few minutes before time wouldn't be a problem. After all, the security was only there to find cases like the one they had in their literal hands. They pushed the man into the back of the van, and then as John, a.k.a Mad Dog, jumped on the wheel, Winston stepped into the passenger seat.

"Don't be an idiot, and don't speed."

There was a reason why they called him "Mad

Dog." The adrenaline and anger shots seemed to have an incredibly strong effect on him, and whenever they went for their weekly shots, John went ballistic. Winston was one of the few who knew how to deal with his moods, and it was just because he knew anger pretty well himself. He had dealt with it his whole life. The fury of everything he had endured seemed to coil in his stomach, and he swallowed it all down, making it small, making it disappear.

"Who do you think I am?" Mad Dog replied as he turned a corner.

If he didn't know any better, he'd think Mad Dog had just made a joke, but no Blackhat was ever going to make one of those. After all, they weren't allowed any emotion vials apart from those that turned them into better soldiers. Blackhats were all either part of the civil police or the Military personnel, chosen from a young age to serve Bellevue and the towns on the outside whenever required.

And that was exactly what everyone at the Academy was talking about at the moment. They were so close to graduation that they were all wondering who was going to be deployed overseas and who wasn't. Bets were being placed on who was going to be deployed, but Winston had stayed away from all that.

"Thinking about deployment?" Mad Dog asked as if reading his mind.

"I was, actually."

"I still don't get why you always think so much about it; you don't have a say in it. And it doesn't make a difference, anyway," John said apathetically. "You bet on it, and then that's it. If you get some money from your bet, great. If not, nothing changes. You fight here, you fight out there, it's all the same… Patrol, get the bad guys, go home, sleep. Repeat." John lifted his shoulders in a shrug at the end, sounding bored as he drove toward the research facility.

Winston only nodded, trying not to give himself away.

He knew he shouldn't care, and he tried to pretend like he didn't. But as graduation got closer and closer, it was harder not to think about it. He was faithful to the regime, and he knew that the only way he could find out more about himself was to be deployed overseas when his training ended. That was why he had made an effort to be the best at everything.

He wanted to graduate, decorated with the most medals possible, so he could become overseas material. Out there, he'd be able to figure it all out: to see if there were more people like him. Handing himself in wasn't an option. After all, he wasn't suicidal.

"Your parents' health okay?" John asked in his usual chit-chat.

It wasn't that he cared, but John liked the sound of his own voice, and liked to have the silence filled up whenever possible.

"Mom's fine. Dad… I have no idea."

"Same, dude, same. Haven't heard a word from my father in… eight years, I think."

Winston's mother was a Gray, which meant Winston had three younger brothers. Most Gray women were to have at least three children, who would be assigned to different tiers and jobs, depending on what was needed at the time of their coming of age.

Winston himself had been taken to the Military Academy when he was only twelve, due to his father being a Blackhat and part of the Military, too. John's case was similar, as his father was a Blackhat, too. He wasn't sure about his mother; he had never asked. Winston's father had been deployed overseas when Winston was only six, and he hadn't heard anything about him ever since. Most people who were deployed never returned, as they went off to fight whatever war was going on at the moment.

And that was what he wanted.

He wanted to go out and see for himself why no one returned. Why no one ever came from the outside of that huge wall and talked about how things were out there.

Was it all the same? Was the whole world an emotionless pit?

He couldn't help but wonder about it; he had done so since he was very young. After all, he had never met anyone else who had feelings — not like he did.

———

The lab was quiet as they walked down the halls with the prisoner in tow. That wasn't unusual, but Winston often forgot how eerie and creepy the place was. He felt cold tendrils sneaking up his spine, and he shuddered.

"You all good?"

"Just cold," Winston said with a shrug. "Didn't put my thermal on today."

"Sucks," replied John.

He knew the halls well, and they took a turn to enter the Emotions Wing. It was right next to the Militia Lab, the one where they went to get their shots every week. Winston swiped his card at the entrance, and at the beep, they opened the doubled doors and signed in at reception. For the past few years, Winston had been to the Fox Lab regularly, just like everyone else on his squad. He usually went during the first hour of the morning to get his shot, so being there before dinner felt odd.

"Prisoner 1287B, found fighting on fifth and fourth," John said to the receptionist as she typed the details into the computer. "Suspected of being high on anger."

The man thrashed a little, fighting the restraints of the handcuffs, and John simply smacked him on the head with a bored expression as the receptionist kept asking him questions.

"How does he declare?"

"I'm innocent, innocent!" The man struggled some more, and John pinched his shoulder hard, numbing him until he was docile.

"Doubt that." The receptionist kept typing, not even flinching. "Okay, all done here. Take him to room four. Lock the door when you leave; we'll take it from there."

"Roger that."

They took the prisoner to room four, opened the door with the magnetic government cards, and shoved him in. John locked the door back and, as soon as it closed, a dense white gas came out of the corner of the room. The man looked at it with wide eyes, but he didn't struggle. He sat on the ground, his eyelids growing heavy, and a moment later, they knew he'd passed out. There was no point in waiting for it, so Winston and John made their way toward the exit.

"New subject to test?" a young girl asked the receptionist as they walked out.

Her hair was the color of fire, and Winston couldn't help but glance.

"Yes. Could you take care of it, Anna? He's already been sedated, should be passed out in a minute. Take the blood sample, and send it to testing."

"Yes, I've done it before. I'll take care of him."

Something in her tone caught Winston's attention, but he tried to keep his eyes on the door. He wasn't sure what it was, but the way she had said the last word, dragging it a bit longer than needed…

"Come on, man," John nudged him on the shoulder, and Winston realized that he was already standing by the double doors. With a shake of his head, he walked out. "What's up with you today? Did you take all your pills this morning? You seem a bit out of it. Are you sure you're not coming down with some sort of sickness?"

"I took all my vitamins, don't worry. Just didn't sleep well last night," Winston lied. "Let's get back to the barracks. I can use a nap."

They got out of the building and jumped back into the van.

"See you in a week, Foxy," John said, waving to the building as if it were a person.

"You know there's no need to be polite to buildings, right? Didn't they teach you that it's only for humans?"

It sounded too much like a joke, and Winston bit his tongue as he realized the mistake in it.

Luckily, John only shook his head. "Just practicing my skills for the day I run into a Bluecoat."

He shrugged nonchalantly, and Winston changed the subject to something boring, like the weather, as they made their way to their base. That way, there were no chances of him messing up.

It was getting harder and harder every week. The closer he grew to his squad, the harder it was for him to act like them and remain a cold and calculating soldier. Winston did care about them and their wellbeing. But no. He shook his head again and opened the window so the cool air would clear his head.

He couldn't care. He couldn't feel anything at all.

CHAPTER
THREE

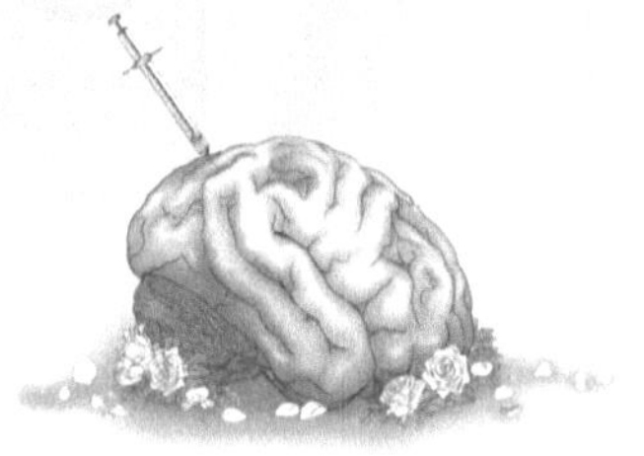

ANNA

As Anna walked toward the holding cell, she couldn't help but look over her shoulder to the retreating soldiers. She didn't usually pay them much attention, but she noticed the way one of them had stared at her — which was highly unusual.

A little curiosity settled in the pit of her stomach, and she bit her lip to avoid smiling.

What if…?

No, she couldn't be thinking like that. Getting her hopes up for a simple look was stupid, and she knew better than to project her feelings onto others.

She pressed the magnetic card to the reader on the door and opened it up. The subject was lying on the floor, unconscious, and she looked at his chart. Prisoner 1287B. No name, no nothing, just a number.

That was pretty much all the lab needed to know; the rest would go to court if the test results came up positive. She took the blood sample in a matter of seconds and went over to the testing lab to do the job herself. Results would be revealed in just hours, and she wanted to be the one to check it out and fill out the report.

———

"Anna, there's something for you."

It had been a few days since her encounter with the tall soldier, and Anna was still thinking about him as her mother knocked on her bedroom door and took her out of her daydream. She knew it was wrong, and that hoping was fruitless, but she couldn't help it. Anna had always been a dreamer.

"What is it, Mother?"

"A letter. It's got the government's seal."

She handed her the piece of paper, and Anna took it with trembling hands, dreading what could be inside.

She knew the odds, though. At her age, she would

be either getting the lab's decision on whether her internship was turning into a hired position, or…

No, it couldn't be.

She was still young; she had at least another year or two before the other letter. Surely, this was just the confirmation of her hard work, and an acceptance into the lab as a hired and permanent staff member. It *had* to be.

"Come on, take it."

Her mother still had the letter in an outstretched hand, and Anna took it with trembling fingers.

Glenn crossed her arms over her chest in a comfortable position as she leaned against the wall and waited for Anna to open it. The girl took a deep breath and turned her face into nonchalance as she tore open the envelope. There was a single piece of white paper inside, and as she unfolded it, her stomach fell to her feet. Anna was glad that she was already seated, because her hands were trembling, and she thought she would have fallen, otherwise.

"And?" Glenn asked, ignoring her daughter's emotional response.

She was either blind to it or had deliberately decided to pretend it wasn't happening.

"It's… a mandate."

"Marriage?"

The word sounded so normal on her mother's lips. She couldn't understand how it didn't taste sour to her mother as it did to her.

"Yes."

It was barely a whisper that escaped between the huge knot in her throat, and Glenn only nodded before turning to leave.

"I guess it's time," she said as she walked out.

Anna stayed there, staring at the words and reading them over and over to try and make sense of them.

Anna Chaplin,

We hereby inform you that you have been selected for the Whiteshirt Marital Program. You are required to attend the marriage lab within twenty-four hours of receiving this letter to provide blood and urine samples.

The union will be arranged in the next sixty days as per protocol, and as declared by law, you'll be expected to be with child before the end of the year, after finishing the fertilization procedure.

A pamphlet will be provided to you at the lab with all the information on fertility you will need to read, the diet to follow, and prescriptions for vitamins. A full guide can also be found on our online portal in case any doubts arise.

Regards,

The Whiteshirt Marital Committee

She felt her eyes filling up with tears and looked up so they wouldn't spill.

"It can't be; it can't be…"

Anna needed more time. She needed time to figure it all out, to understand what was happening to her, to the world. To find a way out.

Trembling hands and all, Anna stood up, crumpled the piece of paper in her hands, and shoved it into her desk's top drawer before heading toward the dresser.

She changed into her usual attire: a long white coat with matching white boots.

With her chin held high, she marched into the bathroom and did her makeup as she did every morning: just a little powder, a little eyeliner, and some lip balm. She willed the tears to stay away, the nausea churning in her stomach to settle, and the fast thumping of her heart to slow down. She stared into the mirror for a full minute, making sure the tears weren't about to spill.

Once she was sure they wouldn't, she grabbed her bag and went to the Fox Lab.

———

"Anna, there's something for you."

Not again, she thought. *Not again.*

"What is it, Alexa?"

"An envelope." Alexa, the receptionist, handed it to her, and Anna willed her hands not to shake.

It'd been just over twenty-four hours since the letter that'd turned her life upside down and put a death sentence on her life as she knew it, so Anna was almost unwilling to open the new envelope at the lab. But this time, she was certain of what she'd find inside. Her internship was about to be over, and the envelope held her future: whether she'd be given a permanent position at the Emotions Wing of the Fox Lab, or whether she needed to pack up her things and be sent elsewhere — to try her luck at another discipline.

Anna tore the envelope open and looked at the piece of paper inside.

"So?" Alexa was looking up at her, wanting to know if they'll keep working together or not.

"I'm in," Anna struggled to keep the smile from extending on her face, and instead, shrugged a little. "We'll keep working together."

"Great, you know what you're doing, not like the other interns. My job is easier with you here, so it makes sense."

"Yeah… Thanks."

"Have you checked on Prisoner A154 already?"

Anna's excitement deflated, and she nodded. "On my way."

She grabbed the folder from the counter and put the envelope away before heading toward the rooms in the back.

It was a morning like any other, following the charts and getting blood samples from the prisoners brought in the night before. After that, she headed to the main lab to run the tests. Most of them came back negative (thankfully), and the rest looked like they deserved their penalty.

One man had been brought in for killing a co-worker after a riot, and another for punching his wife in the face after she served him a cold meal. Anna's stomach churned with disgust, and she filled in the forms, stating that the analysis came back positive, and both prisoners had indeed used emotion vials.

I need to regulate what's going on with the Grays, she thought.

Things were getting out of control, and Anna

couldn't help but feel a little guilty. Grays were becoming addicted to the adrenaline rush they got from anger, as it was harder to come across joy for that fix.

In some ways, the compositions were similar. Both Blue Joy and Crimson Fury had adrenaline and serotonin. But while Blue Joy had dopamine and oxytocin, Fury was laced with endurance and strength drugs. The mix of creatine, caffeine, and beta-alanine created an almost "high" feeling as it kept the muscles going for longer and helped avoid fatigue.

The last case of the day was a young woman, and Anna felt bad the second she looked at the picture in her file. She looked so empty of emotion, like everyone else, dark circles under her eyes, and her skin was full of scratches and bruises.

Anna remembered the feel of her rough skin as she took the sample. The woman was probably a worker in one of the factories, where days blended into one another with the long hours of work. Her file stated that she'd refused arrest, violently, but didn't say anything about bad behavior before that.

Checking the charts, Anna noticed high adrenaline and norepinephrine, as well as high caffeine in her blood, but the rest of her parameters seemed normal… just like how an emotional person would react to a stressful situation.

She noted the woman's number, committed it to memory, and then changed the results, deeming the woman as not guilty.

She compiled the files back into the usual folder and

walked out of the lab. It had been a long day, and it was already getting late, so she walked fast, wanting to clock out and head home to work on her investigation in private for a little while.

The memories from the day before, and her quick visit to the marital department, were still too fresh. She knew she should look at all the information they had given her, but she hadn't even taken it home, still holding it with her paperwork. Distracted as she was, she didn't look up when she turned the corner heading into reception — and slammed face-first into a solid human wall.

"Ow!"

"Sorry, are you okay?"

Anna shook the confusion out of her head and looked up to find a pair of deep brown eyes looking down at her. A few of the papers had fallen out of her folder, and she quickly crouched to pick them all up as she mumbled an apology to the familiar-looking guy.

"Sorry, I wasn't looking. I'm okay."

"Let me help you."

The soldier crouched in front of her and picked up a few of the papers, handing them back to her one by one as he did, his eyes never leaving hers.

"Winston! Are you coming?" another soldier yelled from the end of the hall, and the guy barely glanced up to reply.

"Coming! Wait for me outside!"

Anna glanced back at the retreating soldier as he nodded and turned his back to leave. He was the opposite of the man she had in front of her. While the other man was pure muscle, and as wide as he was tall, Winston was thin for a soldier, his tall frame making him look skinnier than he was. His skin was almost pale, and his short chestnut hair had a golden tinge to it.

"Are you okay?" Winston asked once more, helping Anna to her feet with a gentle hand under her elbow.

Anna then remembered why he looked so familiar. It was the same soldier she'd caught staring at her the week prior, and the way he was looking at her now…

"I'm fine; thank you for your help."

A little flush came up to her cheeks when she noticed the last piece of paper the soldier had handed her. It was the information on fertility that she had been handed the day before, a big stamp from the fertility clinic on the first page. She quickly shoved it into the folder and tried to take a calming breath so her cheeks would stop burning.

"It's okay. I'm sorry for running into you. I should have been paying more attention. I'm Winston, by the way."

He stretched his hand forward, and Anna took it in hers, his warmth spreading up her arm, and her doubts from before multiplying ten-fold.

"It was all my fault for not looking where I was going. Once again, thank you for helping me pick it all up. And… I'm Anna, it's a pleasure to meet you."

"I guess I'll see you around, Anna."

With a nod of his head, Winston walked around her to follow his companion, who was long gone.

"You sure will. I'm here almost every day."

Winston turned around to glance at her over his shoulder, and something akin to a smile flashed on his face for a second before he turned again, and she was left looking at his retreating back.

What was that?

There was no way she had imagined it again: that bright sparkle shining deep within Winston's eyes. It took her a while to turn around and walk back to reception. Once she did and handed all her folders for Alexa to file, she bit her tongue. She wouldn't do it. She couldn't ask.

"Is that everything for today?" Alexa asked.

"Yes… Actually, no," she said too quickly.

"Yes, or no?"

Alexa didn't even look up, her fingers still typing quickly as she started filing the information from the charts on her desk.

She had already hinted at it, and she wasn't going to be able to forget about it, so she thought she might as well just go along with it.

"There's a squad that comes in every week for their shots. I just ran into them heading out, and it gave me an idea for my graduation project, now that I've officially been given the position. Do you think you can print their information for me? I want to look at their charts and see if any subjects might work for what I have in mind."

The lie was easy, and Anna felt guilty for it, but there was only one way for her to figure out if Winston was really who she thought, *what* she thought. By spending more time with him. And not even knowing his last name; that was the best way for her to find out more about him and get to know him better.

"Sure, I'll send it over to your email."

"Actually, can you print it out for me? I'll take it home and start looking at it tonight if that's not a problem."

"Sure." Alexa barely nodded and kept typing. Within thirty seconds, the printer started working. "Just grab it once it's done."

"Thank you."

As soon as the last paper was out, Anna snatched it all and put it inside a folder together with the fertility papers. Shoving it all in her bag, she headed out of the lab and toward her car, which was parked in the same spot as every other day. She jumped in, started the engine, turned on the heat, and took the folder out from her bag.

Her fingers drummed nervously as she scanned the names… until she found him. Heart jumping wildly in her chest, she read his information.

Name: Winston Hitcher
Tier: Blackhat
Mother: Gray
Father: Blackhat (deployed)
Age: 18 years old
Height: 6' 4"
Weight: 182 pounds
Assignment: Military Academy Cadet
Blood type: O-negative
Weekly shots: Crimson Fury, PED, modafinil

Anna read his whole file, her heartbeat an echoing

thrum in her chest as she did. Maybe this was her way out. Maybe this was a sign that there was still hope, that her days were not counted, that she could get out of there, that she could do more than just survive.

When she finally drove home, determination was the only emotion coursing through her veins.

CHAPTER **FOUR**

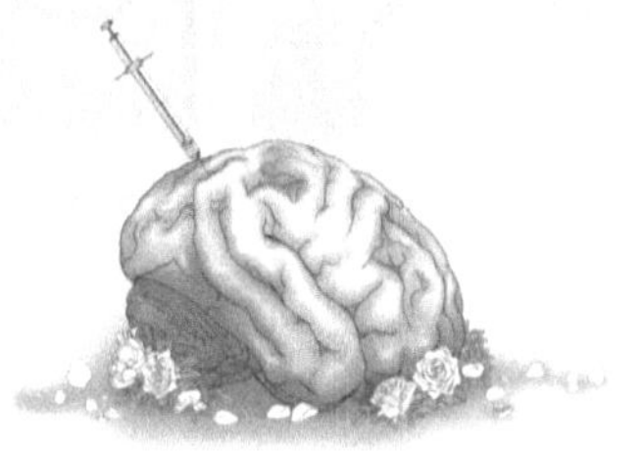

WINSTON

The next morning, Winston got up in the barracks, hoping his week would fly through. The look in Anna's eyes as their fingers had briefly touched while handing her the paper burned his memories, and he willed his mind to let go of it. It was stupid. There was no point in thinking about it. Anna had simply been polite, as it was her job to treat each soldier with respect. That had been all.

"Morning," John showed up at his side in an instant, jumping down from the top bunk.

"Mad Dog, slept well?"

"Like a drugged-up soldier."

It was his reply every morning, and Winston struggled not to snort. Unlike him, who was given modafinil to stay awake, Mad Dog was usually given melatonin to help him sleep. But it was a mild natural drug and didn't usually do much. With all the other pills he took, something stronger would mess up his system, so John simply ran on little to no sleep. He still did all the training as the rest of them, so as long as he wasn't causing trouble, the generals were okay with it.

"Strength training today?" he wondered, already knowing the answer.

"Yup, ready to go?"

"Always."

They marched out of the barracks together, only to run into a general standing outside the door and about to go in. They both saluted, clapping their boots together and taking a fist to their chest.

"General."

"Cadet Winston Hitcher, you're to report to the main office, now."

"Yes, sir!"

Winston saluted again and turned to head to the office, but not before glancing at John, wondering what was going on. John simply shrugged one shoulder, showing him a thumbs up as if wishing him luck.

Winston found another official sitting at a desk in the office, his expression as bored as it could be. He glanced up as Winston entered, waving for him to sit.

"Cadet Hitcher, you have been requested to attend the Fox Lab. There's a new investigation starting, and they need subjects. Your name has been picked due to your response to the drugs being used. I believe there's a new drug they need to test, and your charts matched what they needed. You're to report there this afternoon." Winston knew better than to ask questions, so he bit his tongue. "Report at reception for procedure F25b at the Emotions Wing. You're dismissed."

With a bow of his head, Winston stood up and headed back to the training grounds.

His morning went by in a blur of motions, following the indications of the general as he did uncountable push-ups, climbed ropes, ran miles without end and with a twenty-kilogram bag over his shoulder, and then repeated the whole circuit again. And again.

By the time training was over, and he hit the showers, his every muscle was in knots. He let the cold water run over him aimlessly, untangling the dirt knots out of his hair and brushing the soil from beneath his nails. The whole time, his mind went back to that moment in the office.

Another drug trial couldn't be good. Every time the needle went into his arm, he felt a little less like himself. But it was what it was. It was his duty as a citizen and a soldier to do these trials, so he told that little voice in his head to shut up.

He scrubbed the rest of his body until no trace of

dirt was left. All he had to do was fulfill his duties in society. After all, wasn't that what his mother had always told him?

Do as you're told, and they will leave you alone.

He didn't know how things had been before, as not many changes had occurred since he had been born, but his grandmother left a journal he often looked at when he was a child. She had been born before the vaccines were mandatory and had often written about her life.

After the vaccine had been given to her, the change was obvious, and Winston couldn't help but wonder if it had been one of the things that drove her to commit suicide. It was hard to picture, as the suicide rates in town had dropped to zero after the serum was improved, and the whole town immunized, but still, reading her entries… Winston had always wondered.

She had written a bit about Faulkner before getting the vaccine, and how he had gotten a liking for power as soon as he'd been named "supreme leader."

The serum was meant to make things easier, to guarantee a society where there would be no crime, no hate, and no violence. It had clearly worked for years, as during his whole childhood, Winston hadn't experienced or seen any violence around him. It had been something new to him when he joined the Militia, and the shot had been provided.

He felt it as a kid, but it had been easy to mask it, to hide it. But it was different in the Academy, where they were meant to get angry, to get the Crimson Fury shot and let it all out, punch bags without end, and shoot moving targets. Crimson gave a glint to men's eyes, one that Winston had started seeing in the men around the Grays' settlements during the past few weeks, which was concerning, to say the least.

At camp, they were meant to train to protect themselves from the outside world, not to monitor their own town, as they were doing at the moment. According to the history lessons, as soon as the whole town had been vaccinated, the outside world deemed them vulnerable, and attacks started. Faulkner then decided to isolate Bellevue, to turn it into a small self-sufficient town that didn't need the outside world.

That was exactly why Winston was so curious about being deployed outside of their bubble. It was said that politicians paid well to get Bellevue soldiers, and Winston wanted to know why. He wanted to know if the rumors of the vaccine going global were true or not.

He needed to see the outside world for himself.

———

"Winston Hitcher, reporting for procedure F25b," he told the receptionist amidst entering the lab that afternoon.

The woman typed a few things on the computer, and then looked at him.

"Room 36F, on the left-hand side of the hall, to your right. Trainee, Anna Chaplin, is waiting for you there."

Winston wasn't oblivious to the name given to him, and he remembered the redhead from the other day, wondering if this was a coincidence, and if, by any chance, he was about to run into the same woman again. He thanked the receptionist and followed her indications, knocking on the door to Room 36F only a minute later. His heart was already drumming in his chest, not knowing what he was getting himself into.

"Cadet Hitcher, welcome. Please, come in."

He wasn't sure if he was supposed to mention that they had met before, so he simply nodded and entered the small room, sitting on the bench to the side as he always did when in the lab. It was such a natural response that he wondered after doing it, if he'd done the right thing.

Anna closed the door and turned to him, half of her lips turning up into a small smile before she cleared her throat and pressed her lips into a thin line.

"Cadet, have you been informed of the reason for you being here?"

"Briefly," he said with a curt nod.

"Okay… My name is Anna Chaplin, and I'm a new trainee in this lab. I have recently finished my internship, and as a requirement to being formally introduced into the team, I need to conduct a study on a subject of my choice."

Winston listened, not knowing what to say, so he nodded once more. He was wearing his thick cargo pants and Military jacket on top of a standard singlet, and he felt the sweat gathering in his back and neck as he sat there.

Anna was standing close to him now, a stethoscope around her neck, her hand reaching up to place two fingers on his neck. He wondered if she noticed his fast heartbeat, and he forced it to slow down. Learning to meditate at a young age had saved him from many confrontations, and at that moment, he used every tool he knew to slow his metabolism down as much as he could.

"Your pulse is strong, seems a little fast, so let me check on that."

"Sure."

He squared his shoulders and took a few more calming breaths while Anna turned around to grab a tensiometer. By the time she tested him with the proper equipment, all the measurements came back normal.

"Maybe I counted wrong, seems like everything is perfectly fine. Do you get your weekly shot here?"

"I do, every Thursday."

"Any daily medication?"

"Just the standard vitamins."

Anna marked a few boxes on her sheets, and then approached him again.

"I'm going to get a blood sample. Is that okay?"

"Not a problem."

She turned again while she prepared the needle and sterilized all the equipment, and Winston couldn't help but stare at the curves of her gentle face, the shape of her lips, and the way her eyelids fluttered every other second.

There was something about her. It wasn't that she was beautiful, even though he thought she was. But he had seen many beautiful women before, and none of them had ever gotten his attention. No, it was the subtle ways in which Anna moved. The way her lips were constantly being tugged up, and how she moved her face back to nothingness when she noticed herself doing it. It looked like she was hiding something... in the same way he was.

Winston knew it was dangerous, but before he could stop himself, he started talking.

"So, are you satisfied with being picked to work at the lab?"

Anna glanced at him, and then grabbed an elastic band out of a drawer.

"I am," she said as she tied it around his arm. "Both my parents work here, and this is why I wanted to do it, too."

She smiled then, and it didn't look like those fake smiles that kids were taught to do when they were young. It seemed so real, so genuine.

"What about you? Is the Academy life good?"

No questions ever entailed feelings. It wasn't about if it was what he had wanted, desired, or dreamt of; it was always about the facts. About the schedule, and everyday life.

"Can't complain."

"I will just need a few vials of your blood," she explained as she plunged the needle into his arm, and the first vial of blood filled up quickly.

"Not a problem."

Anna pressed a cotton ball to the spot of the extraction and got a new needle. It was unusual to be punctured more than once, but Winston didn't argue or ask what it was about. He was sure that there was a motive for it. Finding another vein and tapping it with a finger, Anna got ready for the next extraction.

"What about your parents? What do they do?"

Winston felt the usual knot in his throat at the question, but he swallowed it and replied regardless.

"My mother's a Gray. She works at one of the factories in town. She's a seamstress. My father is a Blackhat. He was deployed when I was eight. I never heard from him after that."

"So sorry to hear that."

Anna followed her words with a needle, and Winston tried to breathe through it, to dissolve the knot in his throat, and to think about something else.

Anna pressed another bit of cotton to his skin, and then her fingers softly trailed his veins. He breathed deeply once more, trying to ignore the current of electricity that drove him crazy as her soft fingers kept moving across his arm. His shirt was rolled up, exposing every muscled bit of his arm, and Anna seemed to be exploring his skin as if she's never seen another human before.

He cleared his throat with little effort and tried not to jerk his arm.

"Anything unusual?" he asked.

"Oh, nothing. Excuse me, I was wondering which vein would be better for this last extraction."

Her fingers trailed down to his wrist, and she drew a circle there, then flipped his hand over and tapped some of the veins on the back of his hand. The way she held his hand was so foreign, her soft skin the complete opposite to his roughness.

"I think this one will do."

She looked up at him, a big and wonderful smile on

her face, and he felt the heat in his cheeks, the drumming in his heart. He looked to the door as she inserted the needle, and when she was done, and he heard the syringe being placed on a metal platter, she still held his hand.

"All done."

She patted his hand once more, and he dared to look at her. That bright smile was gone, but the feeling in his gut was still there. He needed to get out of there before he did something stupid, but all words seemed to have left him.

Anna was back at the small desk, filling in some papers and taking some final notes, when the door opened, and a petite girl, with long dark braids down to her waist, entered the office. The girl closed the door behind her quickly and leaned against it. Her eyes opened wide as she saw Winston there, as if she were expecting Anna to be alone.

Winston looked between them, and both girls seemed enamored and out of words for a second, after which Anna jumped into motion and rushed to the girl.

"Sammy, I'm sorry. I didn't know you were coming in today."

Anna glanced back at Winston, and her expression didn't give anything away this time.

"Sorry, Anna, I thought… thought you were alone."

"It's okay, I… I've already run those tests you asked for. We can discuss them after I'm done here."

Anna patted the small woman on the shoulder and opened the door for her. The movement was fast, but Winston's eyes were trained for details, so he noticed the moment Anna grabbed something out of her coat's pocket and quickly dropped it into the other girl's pocket. He saw a glint of blue, but the movement was too fast for him to know for sure.

Anna closed the door once Sammy left and nodded politely.

"We're all done here, Cadet Hitcher. Will see you again next week. Thank you for your cooperation."

She went back to the emotionless human she had been at the start, and Winston wondered if he'd imagined everything that had happened between them during the last few minutes. Not knowing what else to do, he rolled his sleeve down, got up, and nodded briefly.

"See you next week."

"Will see you then."

Winston left the lab, a knot of doubt and a huge cluster of questions swimming in his head.

CHAPTER FIVE

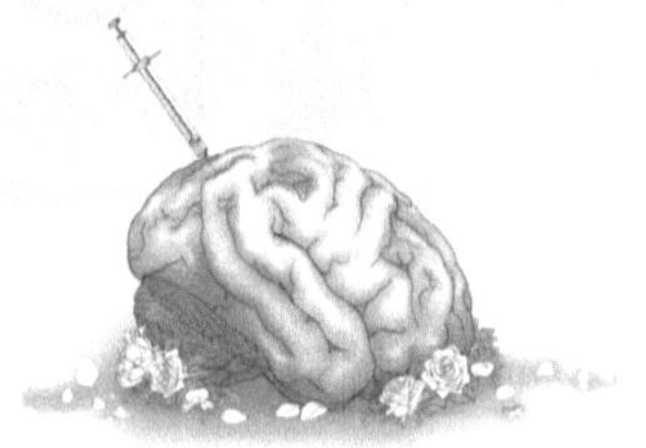

ANNA

With the excuse of the test that she was running, Anna stayed until late in the lab again. She'd been doing the same thing, night after night, since testing Winston, too many wild ideas running through her head.

It was Wednesday already, which meant that Winston would be in for his weekly shot the next day, and in for another test with her on Friday. As she looked at his chart, her heart rate spiked.

"It's not wishful thinking; it can't be," she told herself.

It was the same thing she had been repeating over and over; saying it out loud gave it more weight. No one would have ever seen what she had seen in Winston's chart, because no one was looking for it. She had taken a few different samples, making sure to look for varying emotions in each of them.

When she asked him about his parents, she saw a pattern that showed distress. Thinking about his parents made him sad, which made sense, considering his father had been deployed years ago, according to his file. Anna felt a little creepy looking into all the information available about the cadet, but what else was she supposed to do? After dreaming about it for so long, she was sure she had finally found another human who was like her.

Someone with feelings.

She felt the tears prickling in her eyes and blinked away the dampness. Being alone in the lab was no certainty; anyone could still show up unannounced. Trusting the safety and privacy of her own lab wasn't a mistake she was going to fall into again. After all, Sammy had almost ruined everything for her when she stepped into the lab the prior Friday.

She had gotten her the vial in time, but it had been a close call. If Sammy got caught, then Anna surely would've fallen with her, and she couldn't risk it, not yet. Anna thought about Winston's last sample, the one she had taken after her fingers had trailed the soft skin on the inside of his wrist, and then traveled through his calloused palms. Her cheeks felt hot, and she covered her face with her palms as she giggled.

His dopamine levels had been off the charts on the last sample, and his adrenaline and testosterone levels had also been higher than they should've been.

"Don't be silly, Anna," she chided herself.

Opening the top drawer of her desk, she put the files away and closed the drawer, making sure to lock it with the small key hanging from her neck. She knew the lab wasn't the safest place, but she didn't want to take the papers home, either. She wasn't meant to take files home without a reason to and permission from her superiors.

When she finally left the lab that night, Anna drove home with a silly smile still plastered on her face. She made sure to get rid of it before entering the apartment, and greeted her parents with a simple nod.

"Make any advances on your project?" her mother asked.

"I think I'm getting there."

"What are you working on, again?" her father intervened.

That was the hard part about having parents who worked in the same laboratory as her: lying wasn't as easy. She couldn't just make something up and not have them doubting what she was talking about. So, remembering her plan, she started explaining how she was looking to make Crimson Fury better by altering the proportions of each chemical used in the vial and adding a new component.

"Hasn't that been done before?" her father asked after a moment.

"Not in the same way I'm doing it. All the previous attempts were only about the proportions, while I'm thinking about adding a retro-virus to the mix to also make the effects last longer. I think, if done properly, I could make it so the RNA in the virus attaches itself to the host, making the changes permanent. It would be a single-use vial that would be put into effect by taking a small weekly pill to keep the hormone levels steady, instead of having to get a shot every time."

It wasn't the most solid idea she'd ever had, and she knew it wouldn't work… it was just the lie she was telling her parents to make sure they wouldn't interfere in what she was really doing.

"I hope it works," her mother said nonchalantly.

Anna nodded and went down the hall to her room, where she slumped onto the bed and closed her eyes. She let the image of ripped arm muscles and a twisted sweet smile cloud her thoughts, while a smile of her own tugged at the edges of her lips, making her cheeks sore from how much she'd been smiling lately.

Tomorrow, she thought. *Tomorrow, I'll probably see him, even if for just a minute.*

She wondered once again if he knew, if Winston understood how different he was, and in how much danger he was because of it. Anna didn't know what she'd do if Winston didn't know about his condition, but she had to talk to him about it. One way or another, she had to let him know that she was just like him, that they were different… but together, they could do great things.

When Anna closed her eyes for the last time that night, the image of Winston's attentive eyes was still lingering in her mind.

———

Thursday was a letdown.

Anna waited all day to run into Winston, but when she finally heard that the cadets were in the building, she was called to her boss' office to discuss her project. They wanted to know what she was working on, how she was contributing, and the plans she had for the serum.

She was also reminded of her duties that day when she received the results from the tests she'd gotten done the week prior at the fertility clinic. As it turned out, she was fertile, which meant she had been approved for the marital program.

Her time was running out, and anxiety clawed at her chest for the rest of the day, making it impossible to concentrate on what she was meant to do.

When Sammy entered her lab that night, just before her shift was over, she almost jumped through the roof.

"Sorry for startling you."

"It's okay, not your fault… It's been a rough day."

She walked to the door, her hand already fidgeting with the vial in her pocket.

"Same as last week," she said as she casually slid her

hand into Sammy's pocket and dropped a vial into it. "Any news?"

"They're getting restless. There's not enough *blue* to go around, so they're going *red*. Not sure where they're getting that from."

Anna sighed and rubbed her temple as a light headache made her close her eyes for a moment. *Blue* was the code they used to talk about Blue Joy, the vial they had been smuggling into the Grays' settlements for months. Anna believed everyone should know what happiness felt like at least once, but people had become addicted to the adrenaline rush, and had somehow gotten their hands on Crimson Fury, instead. And she wasn't sure how to fix it.

"Thank you. You should get going."

As Sammy left, Anna turned around and looked at the closed drawer, where Winston's files were hidden. She wasn't sure what she was doing, but it had to be a sign. Why else would she have run into the only emotional soldier?

———

Anna waited at her lab, pacing back and forth as the clock ticked quietly in the corner. When she heard the knock on the door, she laced her hands behind her back and squared her shoulders.

"Come in," she called out.

At the last second, she sat on the chair in front of her desk and laced her hands over her lap, instead.

"Excuse me," Winston said as he opened the door and walked inside.

He made his way to the examination table and sat down.

"Thank you for coming," she said, even though it wasn't part of the protocol. "Having a good day?"

"Busy," Winston replied, one side of his lips curving up almost imperceptibly. A heartbeat passed, and then he casually took his Military jacket off, folded it, placed it on the table, and started to roll up his sleeve. "What about you?"

Anna walked over to him slowly, grabbing a piece of cotton and damping it in alcohol.

"Interesting."

She tried to control her tone, not wanting him to know she'd had a terrible week. People didn't have bad weeks.

She was so conflicted. On one hand, she wanted to scream from a rooftop, tell him everything… and on the other hand, she was doubting herself.

What if he's not what I thought?

But the tests didn't lie. They couldn't. This man felt something…

Winston extended his arm forward, and she gripped his wrist, cleaning his arm for the extraction. She grabbed the elastic band, wrapped it around his upper arm, and then tapped his vein with two fingers.

"Easy, isn't it?"

She looked up at Winston's question, confused as to what he was talking about.

"Excuse me?"

"My veins really pop out. I've been told before that extractions are easy on me because of it. My bunkmate, John, always takes the longest because his veins are really deep, and the nurses struggle to find them sometimes."

He was smiling as he spoke, and the conversation was so natural, so easy…

"Oh, yes, of course. Everyone is different, and you do make extractions… easy."

He didn't. It was so hard to get the needle in. Not because of the veins, not because of his anatomy, but because she was so scared of exposing him. *What if anyone else found the tests she was running and discovered something?* She had to get rid of his samples after she was done with them, and make sure to take his files home, make them disappear. She had been so selfish in her pursuit of truth that she'd missed the fact that she could be endangering Winston.

"Are you okay?"

She had finished the extraction, and she was just standing there, stunned. Her forehead was pearled with sweat, and she could feel herself going faint.

"I'm… yes."

Anna placed the sample on the tray, and then held onto the back of her chair. Her heart seemed to be beating too slow, and dark spots were showing at the edges of her vision. She knew it was stupid to panic like this, but she suddenly felt so scared that she was sure she was about to pass out.

"You look pale… Anna."

A warm palm settled over her shoulder, and she

looked back. Winston was standing behind her, his eyes fixed on her, his eyebrows lowered.

"I'm just a little dizzy; it's nothing."

"Doesn't look like nothing… Here, why don't you take a seat for a moment?"

Winston helped her sit down and then ran to the corner of the room, where a water dispenser sat. He filled a glass with cold water and brought it to her, his hands wrapping around hers as he helped her hold the cup.

"Drink, it'll make you feel better."

His touch was warm and settling, and she felt even worse for what she'd done to him. He wasn't only feeling; he was kind and caring, too.

How had he gone off the radar for so long?

She had heard of a few cases in which people had been immune to the serum. Knowing if these stories were real or not wasn't an easy task, but she'd been getting classified information through her sources for a long time now, and one thing was for sure: none of those people were still around.

"Thank you."

She drank half of the water and placed the glass back on her desk. She closed her eyes for a moment, and when she opened them, she found Winston crouched in front of her, looking genuinely concerned.

"Should I get someone to help? Are you coming down with some kind of sickness?"

"No, no. No need for help. It was just… just a little dizziness, nothing unusual."

The last thing she needed was for someone from the

lab to run tests on her. Winston bit his lower lip, gazed down, and then looked back up at her.

"Is this a side effect of the… tests?"

Anna raised a single eyebrow, unsure of what he was talking about. Winston's cheeks seemed to have turned a light shade of pink as he cleared his throat.

"I'm so sorry. I… saw the papers you dropped the other day when we met… about the fertility clinic. I know some of their tests can have side effects."

Her cheeks heated up so fast that she had to look away for it not to be that obvious.

"Oh, that… it could… it could be. I, you know, I'm not married. I have just been selected for the program, but I'm not paired, yet."

Why am I telling him so much? And why am I stammering?

She had the urge to tell him everything, to reach out to him, to open up.

"Well, congratulations."

Is that bitterness in his tone?

When she looked back at him, Winston was slowly rising to his feet, so Anna placed a hand on his knee, gently pushing him back down so he wouldn't.

"Apologies, I… I don't know what…"

Her eyes found his lips. The bottom lip was slightly darker than the top from how much Winston had been biting it, and Anna wondered, if only for a moment, what it would feel like to run a finger through his soft skin.

"It's okay." Winston's voice was raspy and, to her surprise, he placed a hand on top of hers.

No one had ever held her hand, not even touched her in any way that wasn't strictly necessary. And that's how she knew for certain. That's how all doubt disappeared from her heart, and she did the brave thing: she opened up to him.

"There's something I need to tell you… these tests I've been running with you. They were just an excuse to get you here."

Winston looked confused, but he didn't pull back. His hand was still holding her, so Anna hoped. She hoped with all she had that she wasn't making a mistake.

"I don't understand."

"When I met you in the hall, I knew… I just knew there was something different about you." Winston pulled back an inch, looking into her eyes with caution. "I want you to know that you are safe with me, that I understand… I know you're not like the rest."

She waited for him to say something, to deny it, to pull back. Instead, Winston held her gaze, unmoving. He opened and closed his mouth, then slowly moved his hand back. He was retreating.

She'd ruined it.

CHAPTER
SIX

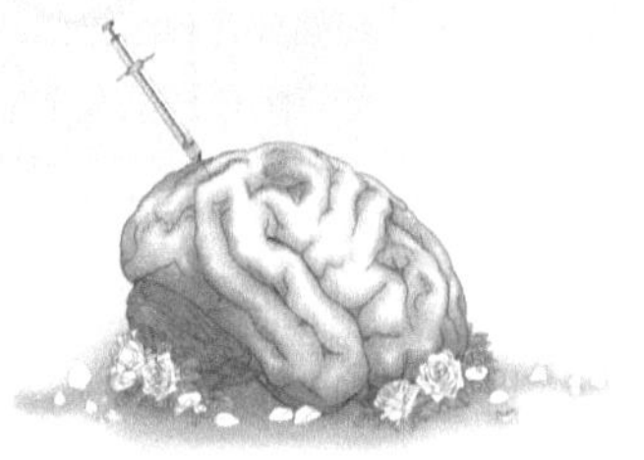

WINSTON

I t couldn't be. There was no way Anna could know that he was different, that he wasn't like the rest of them. Winston's heart was beating wildly, the sound so loud he was scared that Anna would be able to hear it. Slowly, way too slowly, he moved back an inch. And then another. He was about to stand up, to try and make a run for it — anything — when Anna held his hand in hers, her eyes pleading.

"Please, don't. Don't run, don't go. I... I'm not a threat, I promise."

Winston shook his head. "I don't know what you're talking about. All my tests always come back normal. I have no clue what you're talking about."

Lying had always been easy but, for some reason, lying to Anna was ten times harder. She looked at him with a hurt expression, and another thought popped up in the back of his mind. But no, it couldn't be. That couldn't be guilt he was seeing; it was just wishful thinking.

As if reading his mind, Anna smiled.

"Here," she said softly, lifting his hand and placing it high over her chest.

She felt warm through the thin shirt she was wearing, and he stared at her for a moment, until he finally understood.

"Your heart is beating wildly," he said almost in a trance, unable to control what his tongue was doing.

"It's because I'm nervous."

The words were the faintest of whispers. The truth. A secret, a death sentence. Anna was risking everything by admitting out loud that she was feeling *something.*

Seconds stretched into what felt like minutes as they stared at each other, and then he snapped out of it. Winston stood up so fast that he hit the table behind him, the loud metallic bang reverberating in his head. He turned around, grabbed his Military jacket, and put it on in one swift motion. Before he could think about it further, he was walking out the door.

He walked as fast as he could without looking suspicious, and was out of the building within a minute. The fresh air filled his lungs, but it wasn't enough. He felt out of breath, his chest tight, his mind racing so fast that he felt dizzy.

Was this what Anna felt? Like there wasn't enough air in the world to make her feel satisfied? He breathed in deeply using the exercises he had learned as a kid to keep his heartbeat under control. Winston knew he had to keep moving, so he walked toward the Military truck he had borrowed and jumped behind the wheel.

Buildings turned into trees as he got closer to the Academy and the barracks, but his mind wasn't on them. He was numb.

Anna knew he had feelings. Anna could feel, too. And he had run away, like a coward. But it was the right thing to do. It was dangerous to be caught, and Anna wouldn't say anything. After all, he could tell if she told on him. He was safe as long as he stayed away. It was going to be okay. He'd tell her next week that she needed to leave him alone and find another subject for her tests. He'd get on with his life, graduate from the Academy, and get deployed. Everything was fine. Just fine.

"Are you okay? You seem a bit off since yesterday's tests."

John was running by his side, and Winston barely looked at him before nodding.

"Fine, just a bit tired after it."

"What's the test about, anyway?"

"New drug trial," he said nonchalantly.

"Any good? Do you… feel anything?"

Winston's pace slowed for a second before he caught up again. They were doing laps around the camp and still had another eight laps to go before they'd be let free for lunch.

"No, not really. Just tingling."

John seemed a little disappointed as he shrugged and kept on running. Tingling at the tips of the fingers or toes was a common side effect of most of the drugs they took, so it was a safe bet whenever someone asked about "feeling" anything. He didn't like lying to Mad Dog. After all, he was the closest thing he had to a friend. But it was the safe thing to do, and he knew it. His whole life had been a lie.

Ever since he could remember, he had lied about his feelings. Lied about not feeling anything, when inside, he was a mess. He'd been angry more times than he could count, had cried while hiding in his closet when he was just a boy, and had learned early on how to hide everything.

Make a ball with your emotions, and let it drop to the bottom of your stomach. Imagine the emotions dissolving into nothingness, being eaten by the enzymes in your stomach. Let go of them.

He did that again as he ran, the adrenaline from the fast pace helping, even if just a little.

When they finally stopped for lunch, he ate the tasteless food without paying any attention to what he was consuming. Anna's hopeful face was dancing in front of him, his mind unable to come up with anything else. She had been so scared. She'd almost fainted in front of him, probably from the fright of everything she was about to tell him, and what had he done? Run away. He'd run away from her and left her alone.

I'm an asshole.

The weekend went by in a blur between training sessions and, come Monday, Winston and John were sent to the Grays' settlement to patrol.

It was a cloudy afternoon, and Winston had his jacket tightly wrapped around his body and his thermal on. It was colder than usual without the sun, and he walked aimlessly along the roads, searching without really looking. His boots echoed on the almost empty street as he took a turn and found himself in front of a well-known tavern.

Mingo's was a cozy and small tavern where Grays and Blackhats alike were welcomed. It was an unusual place, known for its delicious beer and chill service. No brawls ever took place there, and the owner prided himself in having the best drinks and food in all of Bellevue. He'd visited the place with some of his bunk-mates before, so he decided to poke his head in, just to see if he could get any information.

"Mingo, is everything okay here?" he asked as soon as he reached the counter.

"Business as usual," the owner replied.

"Seen anything out of the ordinary?"

"Nothing at all." Mingo was polishing glasses as he spoke, his expression bored as usual. "We have venison stew tonight if you want to come in for dinner. It's good. I got it fresh from the forest this morning."

"I'll think about it."

Without knowing what else to say, Winston went back outside and kept patrolling. He wasn't sure why that tavern always called to him. Maybe it was because it was one of the few places where he felt safe. Drunk people didn't pay attention to what others were doing around them. It was one of the few places where he didn't need to constantly mask who he was... just as he'd felt with Anna.

No. He couldn't go there. Not again.

Anna was dangerous. Being around her was a bad idea, and nothing good could come out of it. After all, what was she going to do? There was nothing to be done that could make a difference.

"Forget about her," he commanded himself.

———

When Thursday came around, Winston walked into the lab with his mind resolved: he'd ignore Anna if he ran into her and pretend as if nothing had happened. But that was easier said than done. As soon as he was close to the Emotions Wing, he started looking around for her.

Every turn he took, he expected to see her. His heart beat wildly, his palms were sweaty, and every time he turned a corner and didn't find her, his heart sank a little deeper.

He got to the lab without running into her, got his shot as usual, and then walked out, a little deflated. He knew he shouldn't want to see her, but he couldn't help it. Anna was everything he'd been able to think about lately, and he told himself he just needed a glimpse of her smile. Just a second to see that she was okay, that nothing had happened, nothing had changed.

Then he turned another corner — he was almost to the exit — and that's when he saw it: a glimpse of hair as bright as fire.

"Anna," he whispered.

"Excuse me?" asked John by his side.

"Oh, it's, ehm… Anna Chaplin, the investigator who's doing my testing. I need to catch up with her because of my appointment tomorrow. I'll see you at the car in five."

Without waiting for an answer, he ran after the redhead, who was now turning another corner. When he got to her, he called her name again, a little lump forming in his throat as he did.

"Anna."

He felt so guilty for how he had run away, for how he had ignored the opening of her heart. Anna had been vulnerable with him and, in exchange, he had left her alone.

"Cadet Hitcher," Anna said sternly as she turned around.

Oh, he had fucked up. She wasn't even using his first name anymore. Gathering all his courage, he straightened his shoulders.

"I wanted to apologize for the way I acted the last time we saw each other," Winston said almost politely, looking discretely around to make sure no one was close by to hear him.

Anna arched an eyebrow. "Are you really?"

"I shouldn't have left the way I did, and I apologize for it," he reiterated, hoping, with all his might, that she'd understand just how sorry he was.

Only a few minutes ago, he had told himself over and over that he wasn't going to approach her. That he'd go in the next day and tell her she needed to find a replacement but, upon seeing her, all that had disappeared. He needed her. He needed to know more about her, about himself. If she was the only other emotional human around, he needed her help understanding. Understanding what was wrong with him, why he was different, and if there were any more people like them.

"I accept your apology," Anna said, letting a small smile form on her lips for a second.

That simple gesture warmed Winston's heart, and he let the feeling spread through him. She was like the warm sun on a winter afternoon, and he basked in it.

"I'll see you tomorrow, then?"

"As usual," replied Anna, "There's still a few more tests I need to run for my project."

Her lips tugged up, and after looking quickly over her shoulder, Anna looked back at him and winked.

Winked. His heart fluttered, and Winston found himself smiling broadly.

Anna brought a finger to her lips as if silencing him, and he made a huge effort to hide his feelings from his face.

With a nod, he took a step back.

"Until tomorrow."

"Until then."

Anna turned around, leaving him alone in the hall, still stunned.

———

Friday couldn't have come any slower. Every second seemed to drag as Winston waited for his appointment with Anna. He was so nervous, he kept wiping his palms on his pants, his hands perpetually damp with sweat. The early morning training went on as usual, and when it was finally time to get to the lab, Winston was beaming.

He felt like how he did when he was a kid, and his mother would make his favorite food. She never understood why he got so excited over it but, for him, those were the best days.

Walking into the lab with a spring in his step, Winston made his way to the room and knocked before entering.

"Come in."

He opened the door with almost trembling fingers

and quickly closed it behind him. Instead of going to his usual spot at the examination table, he stood there. His back against the door, his heart hammering against his ribcage.

Anna stood at the opposite end of the small room, half-sitting on her desk, her hands laced in front of her.

She parted her lips, and her voice came out as soft as a caress.

"Winston?" A question.

"Anna." An answer.

CHAPTER
SEVEN

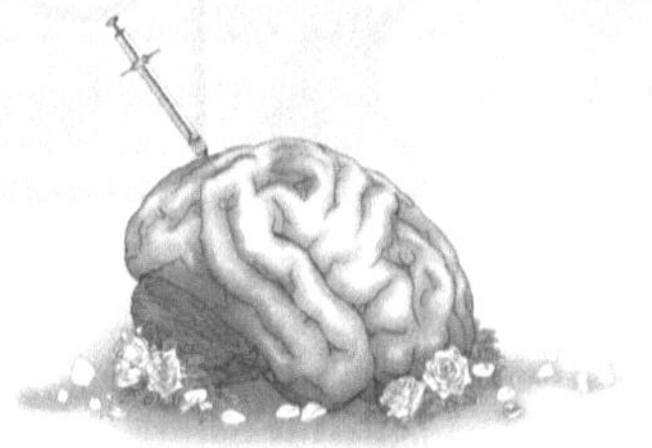

ANNA

She walked to the middle of the room, deliberately slow, while her eyes stayed on Winston's. He was waiting for her, but she didn't know what she was doing, what she was about to do.

"Any tests you need to run today?" Winston asked playfully, a cadence to his voice she hadn't heard before.

After he'd run away the week prior, Anna feared she'd doomed herself. She had spent all week as a ball of nerves, unsure of what was going to happen. Having Winston tell on her wasn't an option; she knew he wouldn't do it for the fear of her doing the same, but she had feared losing him before even having a chance to get to know him.

Learning what it was like to interact with someone like herself was an experience she'd been looking forward to her whole life.

"Maybe a few... practical tests?" she replied sheepishly.

Winston pushed himself away from the door, his lips curling up into a smile, and his eyes full of fire. Anna felt the room charging with energy, and an electrifying feeling that ran from the tip of her toes all the way to the top of her head. She was breaking every single rule she had made for herself over the years. They were going against every natural instinct for survival. But she wanted it. She wanted all of it.

She slowly broke the distance between them, standing right in front of him. They approached each other the way a wild animal approaches a friendly-looking creature: with curiosity, but also with fear of being bitten for making a sudden movement.

So, they gravitated toward each other instead, one of Anna's hands stretched forward, Winston's breaths coming in quick succession. When they were only an inch apart, Winston lifted his arm, grabbing Anna's hand softly between his own and running his thumb through her palm.

"Have you ever…" He broke the silence first, his words a soft whisper between them, "ever met someone like… me?"

Anna shook her head softly. "I haven't. And you? Have you met anyone like… me?"

Feeling. Someone with so much inside of them that they struggled to keep it all contained. Anna wanted to dance, a euphoric feeling taking root in her heart. Neither of them had said it, but they both knew what the other knew — they both recognized each other as equals.

"No, no one."

She observed the way his fingers moved through her hand, and she grabbed his, doing the same. Drawing the lines in his palm with her fingertips, she met his eyes again.

"What does this feel like?" she wondered.

"You tell me," he replied, mimicking her movements.

"It tickles," she said with a giggle. "But also, it's like… I don't know. Nothing I've experienced before."

"Do you… like it?"

Anna giggled once more, a sound so foreign that she barely recognized it.

"I do. You should… take a seat. I should take some samples for my files."

Winston grabbed a seat as usual, and Anna got the equipment ready while glancing at him every other second. There were so many questions she wanted to ask, but she knew the lab wasn't the safest place to do so. She needed to find a way to see him outside of the lab, but was too scared to even suggest it.

So, she didn't.

Instead, she got the samples, filed them, and basked in the simple presence of another emotional human for as long as she could before having to let him go.

"I'll see you next week," she said begrudgingly when he was leaving.

"See you then."

———

Anna's life was always busy. Being at the lab and doing her job, trying to gather information illegally, constantly pretending to be something she was not. But lately, her weeks seemed to only occur for the sake of waiting for Fridays.

For Winston.

That was why on Thursday, when she finally got home late after briefly running into him in the hallway, she didn't notice the letter addressed to her sitting on the table.

"What time will dinner be ready?" she asked her mother.

"In twenty minutes. Have you looked at your mail?"

Her heart dropped. She turned around, seeing the formal envelope on the table. She knew what it was.

"I've already opened it," her mother said unceremoniously.

"Is it the date?"

"Yes, your husband will be here for a formal

meeting in a matter of weeks. They have narrowed the search down to three suitors, and they're waiting for the DNA test results to figure out the best match. In two weeks, you'll meet your husband. In three, you'll be getting married and moving in with him."

She couldn't breathe. It was all too much.

"Okay. That's… okay."

Anna grabbed the letter from the table and almost ran up to her room, moving as fast as she could without seeming improper. Upon closing the door, she leaned against it, her legs giving out as she slid to the floor.

The tears rolled down her cheeks, uninvited, but she couldn't stop them. For a moment, she felt powerless. All the research she was doing in the lab, trying to figure out the workings of society to get out of it, and it was all for nothing.

In three weeks, she'd be married, and they would make her have kids, if she wanted to or not.

But no. She was done with that, done with surviving. She had an ally now; she had hope. And that was all she needed.

Standing up, she brushed the tears away and threw the letter into the trash bin without even looking at it. The next day, she'd talk to Winston. She'd find a way out. It wasn't too late.

CHAPTER
EIGHT

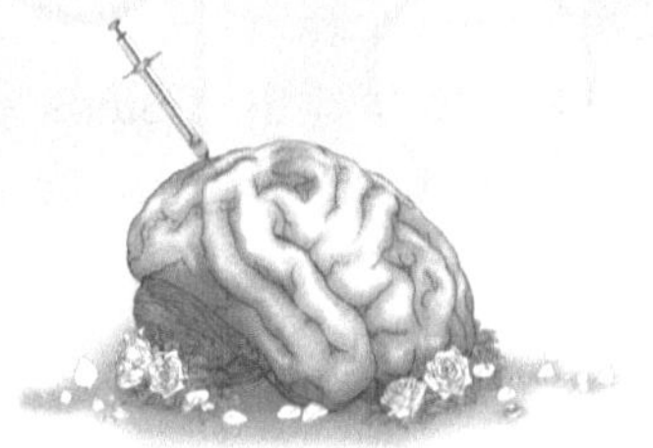

WINSTON

G etting up in the morning, Winston had to repress the smile tugging at the edges of his mouth.

"I hate Fridays," John grunted beside him as he jumped down from the bunk.

Raising a brow, he wondered why out loud. John didn't have any feelings, so hating something was unusual for him.

"You've got the test, which means you're not running with me. My time is worse without you because I lose my pace. My charts look worse, which means they send me to bathroom duty almost every weekend."

"And what's so bad about that?"

"The smell."

Winston suppressed a laugh. Even in a world without feelings, some things could still be physically upsetting, he guessed. He clapped his bunkmate on the shoulder.

"Try to find a way *not* to lose your pace. I'm sure I'm not the only thing setting it when I'm there. Use your watch; you have it for a reason."

The watch that counted their steps and time was a useful tool to keep the pace of their training, but John wasn't great with technology, and that was why he avoided using it a lot of the time. He simply didn't understand it.

"I'll try."

With that, both cadets went their separate ways. Winston jumped on one of the Military trucks they used for everyday transportation and drove straight to the Fox Lab. Once there, he used his magnetic key to go inside. The morning was still early, but plenty of people were walking back and forth down the halls.

He presented himself at the front desk, filled the usual form, and then marched toward Anna's lab. The last time he'd been there, it had been... exhilarating. The softness of Anna's skin still lingered in his mind as he knocked.

"Come in."

He opened the door and found her in her usual spot by the desk. Her hair was up in a pony, her cheeks slightly pink as usual, and the freckles on her cheeks seemed to call him over, to get closer… close enough to count them.

"Good morning," he said in his usual polite tone as he closed the door.

Unsure of the protocol for this new relationship, he went to the table and sat down when Anna didn't approach him straight away.

"Morning."

"Blood?"

"Uhm, yes. Roll your sleeve, please."

He did as she asked, taking his jacket off and rolling his thermal up. Her fingers were careful as she got everything ready for the extraction, and she seemed almost detached from the situation as she took the sample and then pressed the cotton ball to the inside of his elbow.

"Are you okay?"

"Yes, I'm…" Anna looked to the door, and back to him. "It's been a rough day, that's all. Keep pressure on this."

Instead of taking over, Winston covered Anna's hand with his. Their eyes met once more, and he leaned in a little closer.

He had never done anything like it, but there was an ingrained being inside of him that was taking over his body. It was as if he didn't know what he was after, what he pretended, but his body knew well what he needed. They shared their breath for a moment, their faces so close together that their noses were almost touching before Anna pulled back. She turned around, put away the sample, and then sat on her desk chair, rolling until she was in front of him.

Placing a soft hand on his knee, she sighed. "This is so complicated…"

"I know this is all new and unconventional, and…"

"I know."

Anna glanced at the door again, and suddenly got up. Getting to the door in two steps, she latched the lock and returned to the chair in the exact position she had been in.

"I… I'm sorry, but I think we need to talk."

"Yes, of course, you're right."

He leaned in closer so they could whisper and still hear each other.

"I know…" She sighed. "I know we both know about each other, and that it's probably not safe to say certain things out loud. But I want you to know for certain that my intention isn't to tell anyone about this."

Winston knew exactly what she was talking about, and he was glad she was the first to say it. Anna was better with words than he was.

"Of course, I'd never say anything, either."

"You know this is dangerous, right? Us, out in the open, is already dangerous. But us together? We need to be extra careful of what we say and do."

For a second, Winston felt a little annoyed. He wasn't stupid enough to risk his life, not for this, not for anything.

"I know," he said almost rudely, in the monotone he had learned from listening to other people talk.

Anna might have taken it as a bit of a joke because her smile lit up the room.

"I'm sorry if I'm being a little too intense," she said then, placing a hand on his knee again.

He'd never thought another person's touch could do so much for him. That Anna's hand could brighten the world in the way it did. It was almost as if his senses were more invested in his surroundings when she was there, and he was appreciating the way light came in through the small window high up on the wall and danced around, lighting her hair on fire. He could smell the soft perfume she was wearing, and the touch of her hand on his knee was warm and inviting.

"It's okay, I understand. This is… unprecedented." That was to say it lightly.

It was more than that; it was dangerous and on the verge of stupid. It was wrong. *They* were wrong, but together… at least, he knew he wasn't alone. He now had faith that when he's finally deployed, he could go out and find more people like him. Know a little more. He'd fight his battles, but he wouldn't fight them alone, hopefully.

"I was thinking…" Anna leaned in even closer. "Is there any chance I can see you outside of here?"

Winston recoiled.

It was as if a bucket of cold water had been dropped onto his head, and the water was dripping down his back, making his muscles taut, his heartbeat a little faster. The hurt in Anna's eyes was immediate.

"I… I don't know. I'm not sure if I can risk it."

Even though her eyes said otherwise, Anna nodded. "I understand."

He left the lab a minute later with a heavy feeling in his heart. He felt a little guilty for what he'd done, but at the same time… There was no way he could risk it all and see her outside of the lab. It was stupid, and anyway, what was the point?

On Sunday, Winston couldn't sleep. He lied in bed, staring at the roof, and thinking about Anna. The curve of her lips, the cross between her brows when he'd said no. The hurt expression in her eyes, the way she'd looked the other way as if embarrassed.

Monday's training was a hit or miss. He had good sprints when he managed to clear his mind, and then a terrible round as Anna's face showed up uninvited in his head. Guilt was a new feeling in his dictionary, but he was sure that's what it was. It was as if her expression of disappointment was drilling into his mind.

During lunch on Tuesday, he concluded that he'd done the right thing. There was no point in risking more than he already was. He was close to graduating, and within a month or so, he'd be deployed if everything went according to plan. That was everything he'd ever wanted.

That night, he was on patrol, and he convinced himself that Anna was not on his mind. He didn't see her when another ginger woman walked past him, even if she looked nothing like Anna. He didn't see her when a little girl seemed to almost smile at him as she walked past. And he was certainly not thinking about her again that night when he lied in bed, a burgeoning pain within him.

All his resolutions were almost broken by Wednesday, when he woke up thinking that there were high chances that he'd see her the day after during his shot.

Why is this woman driving me crazy?

It was almost as if she was the only thing he could think about.

Disappointment was his only company on Thursday when he looked for her in every corner of the lab and still didn't see her. Maybe if he saw her outside of the lab, then he'd get to spend a little more time with her… just a little. Just as a way to explore his own feelings, to learn about the way she'd survived without being noticed. It was purely experimental. Logical, even.

———

"I apologize if I was rude last time, but you have to understand that with the Military… it's hard for me to get out without being noticed."

Anna had been a little colder than usual while taking his blood sample, almost as if she were disappointed in him. But at his words, she turned around, a bit softened.

"I understand this is not… easy."

"I was thinking…"

He gestured for Anna to come closer, and she

patched up the extraction mark while standing close to his side. Winston looked up, and he thought for a brief moment that having her this close... he could almost kiss her. Just needed to lean in a bit...

"I'm on patrol on Tuesday. I can sneak out after it. We sometimes go for drinks, so no one will question my disappearance for a little while."

Anna's lips were merely a breath away as she replied. "Where?"

"Meet me on fourth and third, Grays' settlement. There's an alley to the side..."

"I know the place."

Winston's eyebrows shot up, but he didn't ask why she knew her way around the Grays' area. No Whiteshirt ever went that way; they were too good to go there, and they had no reasons to.

With his heart thrumming, and his nerves a little on edge, Winston left the lab that day puzzled.

Tuesday at eight — it couldn't come fast enough.

"Mad Dog to Alpha One, do you copy? Over."

"Copy. Over."

It was almost eight on Tuesday, and Winston's nerves were on edge. He was scared, but mostly, excited. He could see Anna out of the lab, really see her. Touch her. Feel her. Know her.

"Drinks at Mingo's. Tonight. Over."

"Not today, Mad Dog. Over and Out."

He checked his watch. Five minutes to eight.

Winston walked toward fourth and got there with two minutes to spare. He could see the dark alley close by and waited until eight to send the command.

"Alpha One, the watch is over. Returning to base late."

It was usually code for when cadets needed to go home to get something from their parents: a change of clothes or to take something to them. Military cadets were free to roam when they weren't on duty, and it was known among the ranks that with the number of drugs they took, with all that adrenaline and testosterone… cadets were usually out all night, trying to ease their calling.

"Roger that. Alpha One, dismissed," came a metallic voice on the other side.

He walked to the alley, and when his feet found the cobblestone path and the lamps from the street dimmed behind him, a hand poked him on the side.

"Hey."

He almost jumped, and he was glad that his reflexes and training were spot-on because his hand had gone to his gun so fast, he wasn't sure how he wasn't pointing it to Anna's head.

"You scared the living hell out of me," he said in an exhale.

"Sorry, Cadet Hitcher." Anna's tone was a playful thing, but she eyed Winston's hand hovering over the gun as she said it — as if aware that she'd stepped too close to the edge.

They almost ran down the dark alley together, and then took a corner down a small street, and another, and another. At first, Winston was leading the way. He wasn't too sure where he was going, but he knew a few areas where there weren't many people, and they could, hopefully, talk uninterrupted. But soon, he realized that Anna was the one guiding him.

"Where are you taking me?" he asked as they rounded another corner.

Buildings were scarce over there, lots of them abandoned as they were getting close to the outer wall.

Anna turned quickly and pressed a finger to his lips, silencing him. She was on her tiptoes, her red hair hiding under a hood, but her eyes bright as the moonlight above them.

"Quiet, or they'll hear you."

"Who?"

"You'll see."

She smiled wickedly, and Winston had no clue anymore what his heart was attempting to do inside his chest. This woman was going to kill him.

In a matter of minutes, they found themselves by the edge of the forest. Anna guided him with such ease, as if she'd been down that track a thousand times. She probably had. The moon was almost full above them and guided their steps, but just in case, Anna had taken a small torch out from her pocket as soon as they stepped between the trees.

When they got to a clearing, the woman finally stopped and removed her bag from her back, leaving it on the grass.

All around them, the trees rose high into the sky, giving off the sensation that they were so far from everything. The stars shone in a way Winston had never seen, and he wondered why he never paid them any attention. No one did.

"What is this place?" he asked while Anna got something out of the bag.

"Just a little clearing in the woods that I found when I was younger."

She pulled out a blanket, and she stretched it onto the grass for them to sit on.

She sat down and patted the spot beside her, so Winston sat, too. He removed the heavier parts of his armor, leaving all his guns and bits and pieces by his side. What was left, was the same uniform that Anna was used to seeing him in.

"Thank you for agreeing to this, it's… weird, but also so refreshing to be out here with someone else."

"Thank you for bringing me to your hiding spot," Winston replied with a twisted smile.

Anna took a little container out of her bag and placed it between them. It was full of small pieces of fruit, and Winston eyed them warily. All the food at the camp always tasted the same, and the texture of fruits wasn't his favorite. He wasn't really hungry either, but he thought it would be rude to turn them down.

"Don't look at them like that; they're not like the crap they give us. They're wild. I picked them myself from this forest."

Winston still eyed them with disbelief, and Anna might have seen his expression because she grabbed a small berry between two fingers and lifted it to him.

"Open."

Winston rolled his eyes but indulged her.

Anna's fingers brushed his lips softly as she placed the berry on his tongue, and he closed his mouth in slow motion as she watched him expectantly. He bit into it, the juices coating the inside of his mouth, and the sweetness of it taking over his every sense. It was like nothing he'd ever tried before. It was delicious. He closed his eyes for a second, reveling in the feeling, and then snapped them open.

"Can I have another one?"

Anna laughed brightly and passed him the container. He ate another one, and when he was about to eat a third, he changed his mind. Slowly, as if approaching a wild animal, he took it to Anna's lips instead. She opened her mouth without taking her eyes off him, and he placed the fruit delicately between her teeth. When her mouth closed, his thumb brushed her bottom lip, and his eyes were glued to the spot as she swallowed — his hand still lingering in the air between them.

In the tense silence that preceded, Winston counted his heartbeats.

Can I approach her? Touch her lip once more? See what she feels like?

He wondered what it'd be like to hold her in his arms, and then, out of nowhere, a loud shriek pierced the air. They both jumped back, and then Anna started laughing, tears running down her cheeks as she held her stomach.

Winston was looking around frantically, his gun already in his hand.

"It's just... an owl," Anna said between the laughter.

"An owl?"

"I'm sorry; that's why I told you to stay quiet before. This area is full of wild owls."

As Anna laughed again, the beating of wings was heard above them, and a white and gray blur flew quickly over their heads — an owl.

"I'm starting to think that you're trying to give me a heart attack."

He couldn't help but laugh then, joining in together with Anna's giggles.

"Sorry."

Anna wiped the tears that were running down her cheek, and Winston found his hand gravitating toward her face again.

He ran the back of his finger down her cheek as carefully as he could. Anna closed her eyes, leaning against the touch. When she opened them again, she leaned against him, placing her head on his neck as she looked up at the stars.

"I hear people used to watch them all the time... Did you know that the stars are so far away, that when you look at them, you look at the past? The light takes so long to get to us, that what we are looking at might not even be there anymore. These stars saw people with feelings. They saw them argue, fight, but also laugh, and fall in love..."

Winston's arm was around Anna's shoulders, and he squeezed her a little — as if saying, "I know."

"Things have changed..."

"But why? Why did they change? To whose benefit?"

Winston tensed, unsure of what to say. Anna's body against him was the warmest thing he'd ever experienced, but her cold words were laced with treason at every corner. And he didn't know what to do about that.

He was a soldier.

He couldn't betray the army for what his heart desired — for Anna.

Could he?

CHAPTER
NINE

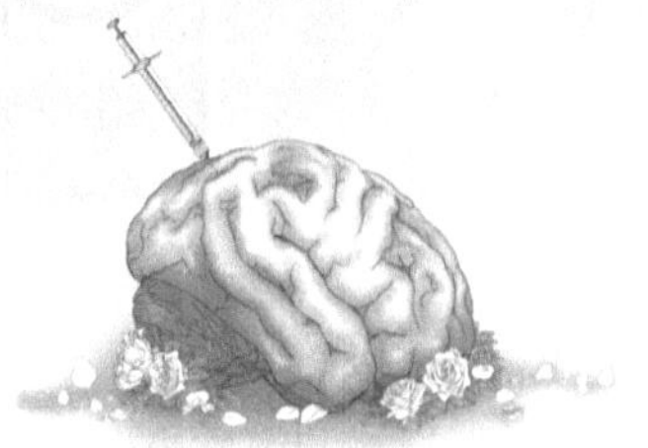

ANNA

Getting used to the new routine had been easy for Anna, maybe too easy. She spent her days in the lab, as usual, but did more work behind the scenes than ever. She was gathering information about the government, Faulkner, and the vaccine as fast as she could. There was a sense of urgency that was making her push herself to the limit.

The time to meet her husband was only around the corner and, any day now, she'd get another letter with the name of her future spouse. Anna knew she'd have to get out before that — or else she'd be stuck there forever.

She found a bunch of papers in the old files that hinted at individuals with feelings, but had found nothing conclusive. Yet. With the help of Sammy, she'd managed to get more Blue Joy vials out to the outskirts and Grays' settlements, and was slowly teaching her how to acquire the samples on her own so as not to raise suspicions.

Sammy was the daughter of Bluecoats, and she was the only one Anna trusted with the truth inside the lab — the government was up to something, and this emotionless world didn't make sense. Even if it's just one vial at a time, she was giving the people back what was rightfully theirs.

And finally, that week, she'd gotten a new lead. She had something to hold onto.

Almost every night, for the past week, she had snuck out to see Winston, even if just for a few minutes. Anna didn't know how to stay away from the sense of high she got every time she was around him. She finally had someone she could be herself around and was learning how to open up, how to let laughter bubble up in her throat, and how to openly feel. It was a whole new experience, one she never thought she was going to have, but one she didn't think she could ever let go of.

Anna felt freer than she'd ever had, like the world

was suddenly lighter, easier — the weight on her shoulder a little less burdening. But she also knew it was only the start. Their lives were in danger, and if she wanted to survive this mad town, she'd have to find a way out.

Figuring out how to destroy Faulkner's regime was paramount if she wanted to be free. If she wanted the whole world to be free, for the serum's effect to be reversed. So, she needed Winston, needed him to help her follow the new lead, so together, they could save the town, maybe even the world. She needed him because he had access to areas that she didn't. Like the waterways.

———

That Tuesday night, she found Winston in the same alley once more and took him over to the forest on silent feet.

"You seem a little quieter than usual today. Are you okay?"

Winston stood by her side as she laid the blanket on the grass.

"I'm okay, it's just… I can't keep going like this. I need to do something else, something bigger."

"What do you mean?"

He sat by her side as he usually did and threaded his fingers through hers.

"What Faulkner did to Bellevue is not right, and you know it. I know it… But the world doesn't know it, and it needs to. We need to do something. Things need to change, Winston."

His face went pale under the light of the moon, and his fingers fell slack in hers.

"You're talking treason, Anna… That's not… That's not why I'm here, you know that."

He was shaking his head, and she wanted to slap some sense into him.

"You and I both know what it's like… what it's like to feel, and everyone should be able to know, too! I don't understand why Faulkner thought he needed an army of emotionless beings, but you and I know it's better… better like this."

She traced her fingers down Winston's arm slowly, and he closed his eyes, his expression unreadable.

He had to understand.

"We're the only ones who can make a difference, Winston. We have to. How are you going to live with yourself if you don't do anything? I don't know why we're different. I'm trying to figure it out, but I know it's what allows us to make a difference. We need to act!"

"I'll be deployed in less than two months, Anna. I can't do anything to ruin that."

She stood on trembling legs, shaking her head furiously. "You can't be serious. This is bigger than you and me!"

"All you're going to do is get yourself killed, Anna. Please, promise me you won't do anything stupid!"

She shook her head again, still not able to believe that she had read him so wrong.

"I can't promise you that."

Anna gathered her few things and shoved them into her bag without waiting for an answer. With the night as her only companion as she rushed back to town, she let the tears silently rush down her cheeks in a way she hadn't allowed herself to in a long time.

———

The young woman was certain things couldn't get worse, but when she got home late that night, she found the dreaded letter sitting on the table. She took the envelope to her room and opened it with trembling fingers.

Inside, the name of her future husband stared at her mockingly. She didn't know who he was, but she had an appointment to meet him the following Wednesday. Nausea crept up her throat, and Anna made it just in time to the bathroom to empty her stomach into the toilet bowl.

She was running out of time.

The night, Anna thought. Thought about how far she had come, how much information she had gathered, and how much she still didn't know. In the morning, she'd get what she needed. No matter what it took, she'd find a way to get out of there. She'd find a way to implement her plan and rid them all of this insufferable tyrant.

She sent coded messages to all her contacts: the Grays, people who had helped her get vials to the minorities, and those who claimed to feel something but really didn't. Most of them were junkies, but at least, they wanted things to change. Unlike Winston, at least a few people were willing to do something.

———

Anna wasn't ready for the knock on her door Friday morning, and had almost hoped Winston wouldn't show up. She was still deeply hurt by his inaction the day before, but there wasn't much she could do. After all, it seemed like it was still her against the world.

"Come in." She tried to keep her voice steady, but it wavered.

The door opened slowly, and Winston stepped in, staying far away as he leaned back against it.

"Anna Chaplin," he greeted her.

"Not for long," she huffed.

She hadn't meant to say it, but the words slipped her lips unprompted.

"Excuse me?"

Anna shook her head and waved for him to sit.

"This will be your last visit. I will let your unit know that our testing has finished. I won't be in your way much longer."

Winston seemed tense as Anna placed the rubber band around his upper arm and got the needle ready.

"I'm sorry for the way I reacted, but you have to understand—"

"Understand what?" Anna snapped, plunging the needle fast into his arm and making him hiss as her cold fingers wrapped too tightly around his wrist. "At least, you have a way out. You're being deployed. I shouldn't have trusted you to help me. Why would you? You'll be out of here in no time." She let out a labored breath as she threw the sample onto the tin tray. "Meanwhile, I'll become Mrs. Thomlinson," she added under her breath.

She turned to her desk and placed her hands on the cool glass while trying to calm her breathing. Losing control wasn't appropriate, and it was dangerous, even inside her own little lab. A soft hand on her shoulder startled her, and she turned around fast, finding Winston only inches away.

"Mrs. Thomlinson? Have they assigned you a husband already?"

"Why do you care?" she asked softly while looking down.

She didn't want pity; she wanted out.

Winston's calloused finger pushed her chin up softly. "I don't want to care, but I can't help it… I care too much. I care about you, Anna."

She shook her head again, unable to believe his words in full. He wasn't ready to leave everything behind for her. He was a soldier, a man loyal to Faulkner, and she'd been an idiot for believing that she could trust him. She could feel the entire world crumbling upon her, her shoulders being pushed down, her chest tightening with the fear of being stuck in Bellevue forever, and not being able to help society in the way she'd always envisioned.

Getting into the lab had only been the first step, and she thought she'd have more time. The serum she'd been working on over the past weeks wasn't ready. She needed time, and a husband was almost like a death sentence. They'd take her away from the lab as soon as they met. She'd have to concentrate on going to the fertility clinic, and wouldn't be able to return to work until she provided the town with at least three children. It was Hell, Hell incarnate. And she couldn't breathe.

"Hey, Anna, I need you to breathe with me, okay? I'm sure you used to do this plenty of times when you were a kid and got upset, right?"

Anna nodded, remembering how, at a very young age, she had to learn how to control her emotions.

"In through the nose, out through your lips. Slowly. Good, you got this."

His hands were on her shoulders, rubbing small soothing circles, his breath mingling with her own as he kept talking to her softly. When she felt better, she managed to look up, finding his deep eyes piercing hers.

"Are you okay?"

Still unsure if she could speak without crying, she nodded.

"I'm sorry that I was so harsh last night. I should've known to put you first, but I just... I've been convinced my whole life that I was the one who was broken. Wrong. And the Military gave me everything. But I... I can't let them simply ship you off to a husband. I can't..."

His hands shook against her shoulders, and she placed one of her hands on top of one of his.

"Does this mean you will help me?"

"Do you have a plan?"

Winston smiled, and something in Anna's chest loosened enough for her to release a small laugh.

"I do. Meet me at the usual spot tomorrow night. There's someone I need to go meet, and then I'll see you there. Now, go. You've been in here for too long, and we can't allow suspicions."

Winston held her eyes a little longer before begrudgingly letting go of her shoulders and slowly walking to the door.

"Tomorrow," he whispered as he walked out.

Tomorrow.

It had only been a couple of days since the new insight had reached her, and she had been unsure of trusting it, but it was time. With a husband less than a week away waiting for her, it was time to take a risk.

————

Anna woke up earlier than usual the next morning, got changed almost in the dark, and headed out to meet with the new lead. Sammy had been the one to point her in the right direction. Somehow, a woman named Valerie had heard about her and the vial trades, and had asked Anna to contact her.

It wasn't unusual for people to enquire about "the trader" — as she was known among the Grays — but this seemed different. The woman wasn't after vials, but after Anna herself. The enquiry had come from mouth to mouth, alley to alley, and she had been asked to go to the local hospital first thing in the morning if she was interested.

So, there she was, first thing Saturday morning, walking to the back entrance of the hospital and slipping into the staff room as she had been told. Unsure of what she was going to find there, she was a little surprised to see a petite, but imposing, woman with medical scrubs on.

"I assume you're the famous trader."

The woman was sitting on a small couch, her posture relaxed. Anna lingered by the door, her hands in her pockets, trying to look uncensored.

"I'm Anna, simply Anna. And you?"

It was a rule to never give more than her name. She didn't often give the real one, but seeing how this woman already knew it, she found no point in lying.

"Valerie. Please, take a seat."

She gestured to the empty seat in front of her, and Anna sat right on the edge, ready to flee if anything weird happened.

Silence settled between them while both women evaluated each other, and then Valerie clicked her tongue loudly and leaned forward.

"I have met many people like you throughout the years," she said.

Anna tried not to express any emotion on her face, which was hard to do at such a statement, "People who are not like the rest."

"I don't know what you're talking about."

It was a swift lie, one that had come out of Anna's lips way too many times. She kept her shoulders relaxed, even though her legs were ready to flee, the door to her side her main point of focus in her peripheral vision.

"I think you do. Look, Anna, I don't have any way of proving to you that I'm telling the truth." Valerie leaned in closer, her voice barely a whisper. "But I know what it's like. I know how it… feels to be so different."

Anna flinched back.

"Yes, that word is… powerful, right?"

It wasn't one that was thrown around lightly. Anna nodded and waited. She wasn't going to say anything incriminating yet, but if Valerie had information, she needed it.

"Would you like me to explain why I contacted you?"

Anna nodded, her eyes quickly darting to the door, just in case.

"I have been meeting with people like you for some time now. There aren't many left, and we're not easy to spot, but between us… there are certain things we see that others don't. Small things that show us we're one and the same. A little flinch, a small tear in the corner of an eye. You know what I'm talking about, do you?"

Breathing deeply, Anna finally spoke up.

"Are you saying that you're… that you have…?"

She let the words hang in the air, unable to say them out loud. It was too dangerous.

"Yes." Valerie smiled, a small but almost adorable smile that crinkled the edges of her eyes and made Anna's heart flutter. After a second, she shifted her face back to nothingness, and Anna almost had to wonder if she had imagined it. "There are more of us, and if you're willing, I can help you get there."

Could it be true? Could this woman be talking about what she thought? Was there really a community of people with emotions, living far from the government and gathering their forces?

"Where?"

It was the only thing she could ask. She didn't want to get her hopes up, but her heart was already racing.

"It's a community up north, far from the government's control. People live there, like they did in the old days, if you know what I mean. I can take you there, Anna."

Valerie smiled again, but this time, the smile stayed on her face. Anna felt her own smile slowly spreading on her lips. Everything she'd been working on, everything she'd dreamt of, might become real.

If there were more people like her and Winston, then she had a better chance. She could gather some forces, mass-produce the secret serum she'd been working on for months. Together, they could make a difference. They'd start with Bellevue, but what could stop them from helping the world? With a community behind her, she could do much better. She could help more people, make a difference in the world.

When Anna opened her mouth to reply, a single word came out.

"When?"

CHAPTER
TEN

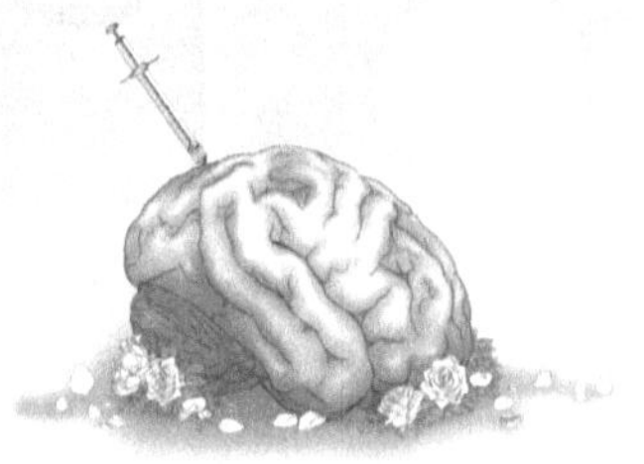

WINSTON

Winston waited for Anna in front of the usual alley, his heart thumping in his chest. John had started asking questions, wondering why he was spending so much time out of the barracks, and he was scared of being caught. He was doing his best to make up excuses every time, but there were only so many things they could do outside of duty.

He was running out of plausible excuses. But Anna was about to be handed to another man in less than four days, and he could not let that happen.

She found him a minute later, appearing out of thin air. Grabbing his hand, she ran toward the woods. They followed the same path they always went down, both of them so familiar by now that they could probably do it blindfolded. Once they got to their spot, they were both a little out of breath. Anna was worse than he was, bracing her hands on her knees, taking in pockets of air and wiping the sweat off her forehead.

"You okay?"

Anna nodded and slowly straightened her back, taking one last deep breath before she suddenly broke into a smirk.

He'd never seen her smile like that. It was such a bright and beautiful thing, and his heart ached at it. Ached to get closer, to hold her against his chest, to see that smile every single day of his life from then on.

She only looked at him, so he broke the silence.

"What's that smile for?"

"I have great news! I… I can't believe it, oh, my, oh! You won't believe this." Anna spoke fast, her words stumbling, one into the other, as she didn't even stop to breathe. "I met this woman. She's… her name is Valerie. And she's part of some community. There are more people like us, Winston. We're not alone! We're not the only ones who can feel. She told me that there's a small settlement to the north, and she can take us there…" She finally took a deep breath, her eyes a little weary as she repeated the last bit, almost like a question. "She can take us there."

Anna's face was as bright as the moon, her smile brightening up everything around her. But still, a little cloud of doubt poked Winston on the chest.

He didn't want to let her down, didn't want to say anything that would ruin the moment, that would wipe that smile off her face. So, he thought. He thought about a way in which he could possibly express his fear without breaking her. Thought about the pros and cons of the situation, and of what would happen if they left with this mysterious woman.

Trust had never been his forte, but he trusted Anna. Trusted her enough to nod slowly, biting his lip not to grin like an idiot when Anna's smile widened — if that's even possible. He couldn't let fear out, not when she was there, looking at him the way she was.

He couldn't let Anna get married, wouldn't accept it, and taking her away seemed like the only way to stop it from happening. So, he nodded once more.

"Is that a yes?" Anna jumped on the spot, taking a step closer so she was right in front of him.

"I guess... Yes, it's a yes."

Anna jumped into his arms, and he caught her just in time, his strong arms holding her as Anna's legs wrapped around his middle.

"Thank you! Thank you! Thank you!"

She followed each word with a kiss to his cheek, his temple, his forehead. Anna was giggling again, and it was so contagious that Winston found himself laughing, too.

"I can't believe we can actually do something, get out of here, show this kind of emotion out in public for once!"

"I can't believe it, either."

He couldn't. It sounded too good to be true, but he had to trust her. It was the only thing he could do. Anna's smile dimmed as she stared at him, her hands still wrapped around his neck, her legs around his torso.

"Sorry." She breathed. "Was this too much? I feel like my emotions overflowed just then…"

She started to pull away, to loosen her hold, to lower her legs, but he held her closer. He squeezed his arms around her, begging her to stay where she was. She was so small, almost weightless in his arms, and he thought he could hold her forever. He wanted to hold her forever.

"No, it's okay… You're okay… And you can stay here for a moment longer if that's okay with you, just a little bit… Let me hold you, feel you…"

Anna's pupils dilated as she looked at him with an adoring smile. One of her hands let go of his neck, and she cradled his cheek. He leaned into that touch, the softness of her palm like nothing he had felt before. His eyes closed, his heart beating so loudly that he knew she could probably hear it.

He felt the soft pressure of a finger trailing his bottom lip, and he let his eyes flutter open once more.

"May I?"

Anna's question was a small whisper, one full of longing and adoration.

"You may," he said simply, his voice a little hoarse, a little rough.

She closed the distance between them, her lips the most delightful thing he'd ever tasted.

———

He watched Anna as she stared up at the stars, admiring how they reflected on her eyes.

They were lying on their usual blanket, their legs half tangled together, their hands held with their fingers intertwined and sitting across Anna's stomach. They had been like that for a little while now, and he didn't want to break the moment, but he had to.

"What's the plan, then?"

They had gotten too distracted in each other's arms, but it was time to go. They couldn't stay in the forest forever, and before they left, they needed to have a solid plan. Anna turned her face to look at him, her smile not as confident as it had been earlier.

"I spoke with Valerie for as long as I could, but time was short as we couldn't risk getting caught. She told me to pack light and meet her by the hospital parking lot at sunset in two days. She'll smuggle us on one of the ambulances when she's going out on her rounds, and from there, we'll transfer onto an untraceable car that she'll have waiting for us just outside of the city. She said she'll be with us every step of the way, that someone will take the ambulance back so there's no suspicion. Said she's been doing this for a while, that it was safe."

"But you still sound worried. Is there something else you're not telling me?"

Anna bit her lip, and her shoulders slumped.

"After speaking with her this morning, I went to the lab for my usual shift. I wanted to find something, anything that could help me get more relevant information that we could take to these people, something that would make a difference. If there are more people like us — hiding — then I want to be able to help them, too. I broke into the company's server, and—"

"You, what?!"

He let go of her fingers, staring at her in disbelief. How could she do something so blatantly dangerous?

"It's not the first time I did it. Don't worry." She patted his hand and held it again, rubbing her thumb on his palm. "There's no way I'm getting caught for it."

"That was dangerous and stupid, Anna." He tried to control his rage and speak calmly, but it was hard when he knew she was going around risking her life. "Why would you do something like that when you're finally so close to getting out? Isn't that what you've always wanted, to get out of here?"

"I do, but I also want to help other people. There's no point in getting out if I'm the only one doing it. And I don't want to live my life hiding. I already do that here." She reached out and grabbed his hand again. "And don't worry about me, okay? I've been doing this for a long time. I've been tapping into their network, stealing vials from the lab…"

She let the words linger, as if waiting for him to move away from her again.

"You did what?" He couldn't believe it. Well, actually, he could. What he couldn't believe, was that he hadn't realized it before. The vial he saw her dropping into Sammy's pocket that first time in her lab, the rumors, the way she always looked so sneaky, how she knew the alleys like the back of her hand, it was all making sense now. "You're the one getting the vials to the Grays?"

She didn't even flinch. "Yes."

"Why?"

It was the only thing he could ask. He understood the rest, wanting to help. But why make them violent? Why get them in trouble?

"Because they deserve it. They deserve to feel something, to know what they're missing out on. I wanted them to feel, to give them a reason to want more than what they have…"

Some of that made sense, but… "But why give them Crimson Fury?"

"I never did. I mostly got them Blue Joy, but I think a small shipment of Crimson Fury was smuggled out right under my nose. That wasn't me. I think it was all a plan by the government to arrest people and get some troubled workers out of the way. I think they targeted people they suspected of having feelings. But it's just a theory. I can't be sure… There's something else I found when I got into the system today…"

"What is it?"

He didn't know if he could take any more; it was a lot, but they were running out of time. She moved closer, almost as if not wanting anyone to hear what they were talking about. But they were in the middle of the woods, the trees their only companions.

"I found some information regarding the vaccine, something that helped me with a project I'm working on, a serum I've been developing in hopes of counteracting the effects of the original, but it wasn't only that…"

He wanted to ask about how she was working on a cure on her own. He couldn't believe his ears, but after all, Anna was fierce. He knew she was a force to be reckoned with the first time he saw her crimson hair whipping around as she walked, the first time he admired the way in which her hips swayed when she moved, her chin held high. But Anna was still talking, so much information being dumped on him that he was struggling to keep up.

"I also found several mentions of a place called North Camp. I'm not sure if this has anything to do with the settlement that Valerie had spoken to me about; it could just be a coincidence. But I think it could also be that Faulkner is aware of the settlement and is trying to do something to get rid of those people. It almost seems too coincidental that Valerie found me now, now that I have you, and now that I'm finally so close to getting my sample of the serum finished. But… I don't know. I have this gut feeling telling me that if I don't try, I will never know. We still have two days; maybe that's enough. Maybe I can print out all the information I found, look at it, find something else that will help us. Maybe I can get the serum done by then."

He waited for a single heartbeat before replying,

wanting to make sure that she knew his decision was final, and that he was sure of what he was doing.

"Whatever you decide to do, I will follow your lead. I don't know if I like how this all sounds, but there's no way I'm letting you go with Valerie alone. So, if you're in, I'm in."

Another truthful smile spread on Anna's face, and he couldn't help but mirror it. She leaned in, pressing her forehead against his. He breathed in her scent, the smell of lilacs mixing with the perpetual aroma of alcohol and sanitizer that was always around Anna. She smelled the same way her lab did, but he didn't mind it. He actually liked it.

"Do you think we can do this?" she asked after a minute of silence, their foreheads still touching.

"Together, we might be able to do just about anything."

He didn't know where that answer came from, but deep down, he believed it. He believed that there wasn't a single thing he couldn't do with this woman by his side. She was his muse, his reason to push forward, to do better, and the only reason he would go against the government.

Without her, he would've never been where he was now. He'd be thinking about graduation and stressing about getting deployed.

Now, he was stressed about running away, about risking their lives for something bigger than themselves. But for Anna, for Anna, he'd do it. He'd put his life on the line, do whatever it took.

They stayed under the trees for as long as they

could, holding each other, basking in a kind of intimacy they had never experienced before. And when it was time to go, Anna kissed him goodbye, the promise to see him again in the parking lot of the hospital being the only reason he managed to walk away from her.

CHAPTER
ELEVEN

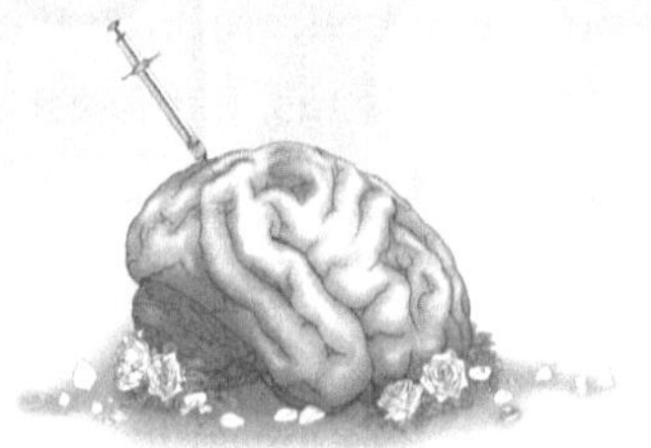

ANNA

Heart beating wildly in her chest, Anna arrived at the parking lot precisely as the sun was setting over the horizon, a bright orange ball of fire barely visible between the tall buildings. She lingered on the outskirts of the parking lot, a small, but heavy, bag slung over her shoulder.

Saying goodbye hadn't been an option. She told her

mother that she needed to take some files back to the lab, and simply walked out the door. Her escape bag had already been packed in the car since the morning, as she didn't want to risk anyone seeing it.

Anna looked around, waiting for a Military van to pull up at any minute. She knew Winston was probably going to be in one. After all, his camp wasn't close to the hospital. She felt as if she wasn't breathing as she waited, her head light and dizzy.

What if he doesn't show up?

She brushed the thought away from her mind the minute it popped up.

Winston will be here. She was sure of it.

When Valerie walked out through the back door and jumped onto one of the vans, her heart went wild. Her pulse was audible in her eardrums, cold sweat clinging to her whole body. The bag over her shoulder felt as if it weighed a ton.

Valerie started the engine, and the lights flickered twice.

It's the signal.

She looked around, her throat closing. And then, there, at the edge of the lot on the opposite side, another flash of lights. A Military van started up, drove a few meters, and parked next to the medical vehicle.

He made it.

Anna almost ran to the van, opened the back door, and jumped in. Winston stepped out of his vehicle and jumped in right behind her. Breathless, she held his hand, and he squeezed it back as he closed the door.

"Ready to go?" Valerie asked from the front seat, looking at them through the rear-view mirror.

"Good to go," Anna whispered back.

The engine roared, and the van slowly pulled out of the parking lot, as if it were just another night of usual rounds. The streets were busy enough, people going back home from work, a few full buses around them.

Anna and Winston lowered their heads and sat on the floor, their hands never breaking contact. She needed that steady pulse against her fingers to know that Winston was there with her.

"Stay low; we'll be out of the city in an hour."

They hummed an agreement, and Valerie kept driving, her eyes always on the road. She looked unconcerned, as if she wasn't smuggling them out. As if nothing out of the ordinary was going on.

"Are you okay?" Winston whispered in her ear a few minutes later.

"Good," she replied, finally setting her bag onto the floor.

It made a loud thump, and Winston raised a brow at her.

"I thought we were supposed to pack light."

"It'll be light once I read through all of these papers, commit them to memory, and burn them," she replied with a smug smile.

"Papers?"

"Yeah, I took a bunch of files from the lab before leaving."

She undid the zipper and pulled the first yellow folder out of the bag. She flicked through the pages, unsure of what she was going to find inside. These were highly classified files, something she couldn't have taken out earlier without risking being exposed.

But now that they were out, it didn't matter anymore. Authorities would surely find out that she was gone in the morning, and she knew she was never going back. It'd mean certain death.

Anna moved closer to Winston, talking in a whisper so Valerie couldn't hear them.

"Should I tell her that I read about North Camp in the files?"

"I don't know. Maybe we can keep that one out. She's only one woman, and I'm sure I can take her down if it comes to it, but I don't think we should risk it, at least, until we get there. Let's see where she's taking us, and then we can decide."

"Okay."

She traced circles in his palm as she opened the file on her lap and started to slowly go through each page in front of her.

Soon enough, a repeated word started to pique her interest. There were a lot of personal files in between what she had pulled out: people who lived before their time, some of them their age, some of them older, some younger. Way younger. Some were marked as deceased, some without enough information to know for sure. But there were too many deceased children, and Anna's stomach was starting to feel uneasy — and it wasn't the motion sickness.

"Look at this," Anna said, pointing at the red stamp

on the file. "I've been seeing this in a lot of files, but haven't found the meaning yet."

"Aberration?" Winston read the bold red word out loud as a question. "What do you think it means?"

"I'm not sure, but if my gut feeling is right… I don't like this."

"Let me help you." Winston grabbed another file, and together, they started to classify the pile into personal files and informational ones. The red stamp with the word "aberration" kept appearing, and all those people were marked as deceased. Anna's gut was twisting with concern, and she didn't like the look of any of it. Between the stacks, a blue folder caught her attention. She opened it, looking through reports and essays.

With further investigation, we have determined that not everyone is susceptible to serum PX320 as originally expected. A few individuals have been immune to it, the immunity not traced to any genetic marker or phenotypic characteristic. The cause of this immunity is unknown, but subjects have been tested and proven to be immune at different levels. Some of them only show certain patterns of behavior, while others seem to have a full range of emotions. These individuals have been classified as "aberrations."

Anna felt the sweat gathering on her lower back, and she nudged Winston.

"Read this."

She passed him the file, and he read it with his brows tucked together, his expression looking more and more worried each second.

"They know about us; they're aware that we exist."

"Are you talking about the government?" Valerie asked from her seat, quickly glancing at the mirror.

"Yes, they know that there are people like us," Winston repeated.

"Of course, they do. They're not *that* useless."

"Did you know that they classify us as aberrations?" Anna asked, unable to hold her tongue any longer.

Valerie didn't even flinch at the word. "I've never heard of that term before. Where did you get it from?"

"Some files I got from the lab before leaving. They're classified reports from the highest functionaries in the Fox Lab. The word "aberration" has popped up many times now."

"That's interesting," Valerie muttered. "We're almost there," she added louder. "We're going to stop here for the night and move first thing in the morning. We're far enough from the city; this place is safe."

"Where are we?" Winston asked, peeking out of the window.

It was dark outside, but the moon illuminated enough for them to see a small facility a few meters ahead. It was a building with plain white walls, tattered and worn by the years.

"It's an old research facility; it's been abandoned for a long time."

When Valerie parked, and they departed the van, Anna could see that the place was deserted. There wasn't a single soul around, only a worn-out road leading to the building, and a thick forest stretching all around it. It was sheltered from peering eyes, so Anna thought it was smart for the resistance to use such a place as their own.

She slung her bag over her shoulder again and walked next to Winston for a bit before he helped her with the bag, a gentle smile on his face.

"I can take that for you," he offered.

It wasn't necessary, but it was a nice gesture, so she let him.

Valerie guided them to a door on one side, which she opened with a key she pulled out from her coat pocket. Inside, the facility was almost vacant. Most of the equipment had been taken away, the worn-out marks on the floors and walls still visible. It was freezing inside, the windows so small and high up that the sun probably never got in. She shivered, and Winston wrapped an arm around her shoulder.

"What's the plan?" he asked, addressing Valerie.

"We'll get some wood to get a small fire going, and then get some sleep. In the morning, we keep going. It's too dangerous to drive through these roads in the dead of night. No one does, and it would be suspicious. But once the sun is up, no patrols will be in this area, so it'll be safe."

They nodded, and Winston got a small sleeping bag out from his pack, unraveling and putting it onto the floor. It was a very compact sleeping bag, and Anna was so happy to see it that she sighed in relief. She hadn't thought to bring a blanket, as it would have been too bulky. But the army had always had the best equipment.

Winston smiled and nodded at her, as if giving her

permission to grab a seat on it. She sat down, her legs crossed, and pulled some folders out of her bag straight away. There were still a few blue folders for her to go through, and she wanted to use the little moonlight they still had left.

"Is it okay if I start on this?" she asked, looking up at Valerie and Winston.

"Of course. I can go get the wood," Valerie offered.

She didn't have a pack, so there was nothing for her to get rid of before walking the few steps back to the door. Winston placed his bag onto the floor, and he was about to sit by her side when Valerie looked over her shoulder, her hand on the doorknob already.

"Big guy, would you give me a hand? There's only so much these tiny ones can carry," she said, showing her palms.

She smiled at him, and Anna almost felt a pang of jealousy at the way she looked at Winston. As if he was a prize or something.

Winston shared a look with her before agreeing, making sure she didn't mind being left alone for a moment. Before getting up, he pressed a sweet kiss to her temple, making her insides melt into a pile of goo, and then he took off his jacket and placed it over her shoulders.

"Be back in a minute," he murmured against her skin.

Anna returned to the files, pulling her arms into the sleeves of the jacket and losing herself in the information. Her nose was almost pressed against the paper, the letters barely visible in the near darkness.

It is impossible for the government to know who is a proper member of their caste, and who is an aberration in the early stages of life. Kids are unpredictable, and some of them do cry and show small signs of emotions in their early years before they're fully developed. If a kid still shows signs of emotions by the age of seven, tests are run, and the subjects are eliminated if the test results come back positive. Aberrations must be eliminated as soon as possible.

Anna felt bile crawling up her throat, but she made herself keep reading. She couldn't believe everything that was going on behind the shadows, and she had never known. For a moment, she wondered if her mother knew. If that's why she had paid such close attention to her as a child.

She shook her head, getting rid of the thought. It wasn't time to be thinking about family, a family that wouldn't even miss her now that she was gone. She flipped the page, and then pulled the sleeves of the jacket over her cold fingers as she kept on reading.

Only a very small percentage of aberrations grow to become full adults. In this case, an agent is sent to infiltrate them.

Anna's heart rate doubled.

Redwatchers will usually pose as a member of their caste, pretending to be aberrations too, in order to get these emotional beings to trust them in full. Redwatchers are the government's newest acquisition, running under serum PX550, a newer and deadlier combination that produces the most advanced and deadly soldiers.

Valerie's cold smile made an appearance in her mind, and Anna shuddered, reading the last sentence with difficulty as the paper shook in between her trembling fingers.

Redwatchers will earn the subjects' trust as fast as possible, drive them to a desolate area, and kill or capture them one by one.

The words blurred as Anna's world stopped. Desolate area. North Camp.

They were in danger. In mortal danger. Without time to come up with a plan, Anna stood on trembling legs. She ran toward the door. A pipe was leaning against the door, so she took it. She turned the doorknob with trembling fingers. Adrenaline rushed through her system. Even if she wasn't ready for what was to come, she knew she had no other option. Winston was in danger, so she'd do whatever it took to help him.

CHAPTER
TWELVE

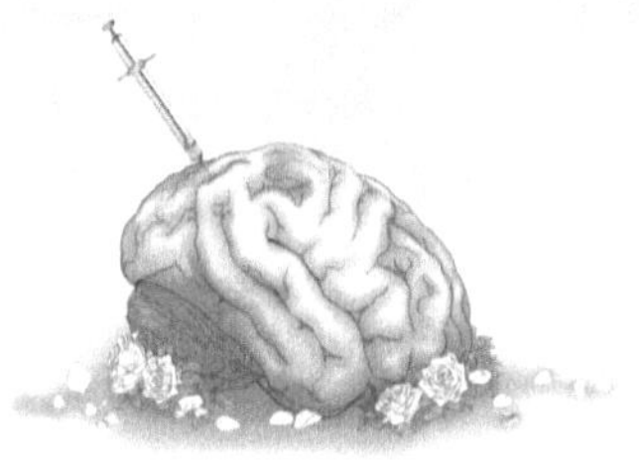

WINSTON

As soon as they stepped out of the building, the air around Winston felt hotter. It had been so cold inside — as if no one had been in there for centuries. Which was probably the case.

He was glad he'd left his jacket with Anna; she'd looked so cold and worried. He really hoped that they were doing the right thing. For her, Winston would go to the end of this damn world if needed.

When did it happen? When had she gotten tangled so deep into my soul? Had it been when she'd held me in her arms a few days back? Had it been the first time I'd tasted her lips? The first time I had looked into her eyes?

He didn't know, but he didn't think it mattered anymore.

Picking up a log and looking back at Valerie, he thought about the road that had gotten them there. He wasn't sure if he could trust the woman yet, but at least, they were in a deserted enough spot for him to notice if anyone came up the road. After all, it was the only way in.

They lingered at the edge of the forest, Valerie picking up some of the smaller branches to start the fire while he tried to find bigger chunks that they could use.

"An axe would've been helpful," he joked.

"It would've," Valerie answered, her tone dull and bored.

He could hear her a few steps behind him, and he glanced over his shoulder, seeing her kick a small branch with the tip of her combat boot, and then crouching to pick it up. Her pants rode up as she lowered to the ground, and the way her boots shone made something in Winston's stomach churn. He knew that gleam all too well. After all, he saw it every single day when cleaning his uniform.

Something isn't right.

"I think this is enough to start a small fire; we should get back," he offered, trying to sound casual.

He eyed the building, thinking of Anna inside. He'd rather keep this woman away from her, but if he could get to his pack, then he could get his gun. He wasn't sure who this woman was, but his gut wasn't usually wrong. Those boots were Military provided, and if she had them, she'd either killed someone for them or was working for the government herself.

He'd have to act fast before she suspected something, just in case she was armed. He couldn't see any obvious weapons, but her coat was big, and she could be hiding pretty much anything in there.

"Sure, we'll come back for more in a minute," Valerie replied.

Winston smiled, a fake and small thing that made him feel sick. He didn't want to smile at this woman, but he didn't want her to doubt him, to realize that he was already planning a way out of there — that he needed to get rid of her.

He walked two steps closer to the building. The back wall wasn't far, but they'd still have to go around the corner to return through the door they'd come out of. Pulse quickening, he took another step. It almost felt as if the world was moving in slow motion. Valerie tripped, the twigs in her hands falling onto the ground with small rattling noises. Out of instinct, he reached out to catch her, his own logs falling.

That was his first mistake.

The second his hand closed around her upper arm, Valerie spun in the air, her free arm swinging in a wide circle and clipping him on the chin. It'd all been an act. The blow made him stagger backwards, white dots clouding his vision. Valerie seemed to be made out of air as she pushed forward, moving with the speed of a gazelle.

Another fist to the jaw, and Winston's guard was finally up. He dodged the third strike and threw a hook. But she was too fast.

The woman dodged again, and her leg swiped down, hitting his legs and throwing him onto the ground. Air rushed out of him in a loud hiss. Valerie didn't give him time to try and get up. She was on him in a second. Her legs pinning his torso and legs, her hands going to his throat. The incredible strength with which she squeezed made his vision blurry at the edges. His hands flew to her arms, trying to pull her away.

Who is this woman?

But he wasn't going to get an answer. No air was flowing down his pipes, and he needed to act fast if he didn't want to pass out. One hand pushed Valerie away as the other tried to reach his boot. He had a knife there, and if he could get it, he could have the advantage. Maybe.

"You're done for, darling! And your woman is next."

She spat the words at him, and he pushed harder, his finger digging into her right eye socket. Valerie grunted, pulled her head back. And then, her head was busted to one side.

Anna stood behind her, a pipe in her hands. She'd just swung it like a bat, smacking Valerie on the side of her face. Winston used the distraction to punch her hard enough to get her off him. Anna swung again, her eyes wide in terror as she got Valerie on the shoulder. The woman rolled to the side, and Winston staggered back an inch, getting back to his feet with some effort and pulling the knife out of his boot.

"Winston…"

He didn't get to answer Anna's scared eyes.

That was his second mistake. He'd underestimated Valerie's strength and speed. Valerie jumped to her feet and lurched toward Anna, going for her throat as well.

"No!" It was almost a breathless scream as he ran toward both women.

He slashed at her back, but Valerie didn't even flinch. He stabbed her between the ribs, getting her kidney. She barely squirmed and kept on squeezing Anna's throat. The pipe had been dropped to the ground, slightly bent. He picked it up and swung. Valerie toppled to the side, blood pouring out of a gash on her forehead. Anna struggled to breathe, and he was by her side in a second, helping her to her feet while she coughed and panted.

"Come on, love, we gotta move."

He picked her up from under her armpits and half carried her weight as they rushed back into the building.

"She's… she's a Redwatcher… highly trained Military…"

"I sort of figured that out. Save your breath; we'll be safe in a minute."

He needed to get inside, get to his gun, just in case Valerie wasn't completely out of the game. It had been a strong blow, but if she was built stronger than a normal soldier, he didn't think that would've been enough. He was pretty sure John would've survived that hit if he were high enough on Crimson.

They got to the door and rushed in. Anna was running now, almost completely recovered. She grabbed her pack at the same time as he grabbed his. He went straight for the gun, keeping it in his hand.

"Are you okay?" asked Anna.

"I'm fine. Are *you* okay?"

"I think so…"

"Stay behind me, please."

Anna did as he told her and lingered behind his shoulder as he inched toward the door. Inside, they probably had the advantage. There were places to hide, more shelter, and only one way in. But outside, Anna could get a chance at running away if Winston got tangled in a fight.

So, outside it'd be.

"If I get trapped into a fight, I want you to run, okay?" He looked at her for a second, her eyes filled with concern, her eyebrows lowered. "Please."

Anna nodded begrudgingly. He risked a second of valuable time to plant a kiss on her temple, and when he turned back to the door, a shadow lingered on the threshold.

"So romantic; that's the word for it, right?"

"You picked the wrong humans, Valerie." Winston shifted to cover Anna completely.

"Oh, I think I picked you perfectly."

There was blood covering her face, the front of her clothes, her hands. But she looked unphased by it.

There was no emotion in her words, either, only a hint of disdain, probably an effect of the adrenaline that she was running on. He had no time to think; he needed to act. Raising his gun and damning any small chance he had of ever returning to the Military, he shot twice. He got her right on the chest. Valerie staggered back, took a hand to her abdomen… and then straightened.

His heart dropped. It was worse than he'd expected. He had no clue what kind of drugs she could be on, but she wasn't even human anymore.

She ran straight toward him. He shot again. He wasn't sure if he got her that time, her body slamming against his like a bull. She tried to pin him to the ground, but he rolled.

"Run!" he yelled at Anna.

They rolled onto the floor, kicks and punches being thrown indistinctly as they wrestled. He thought he saw Anna's shape moving toward the back wall on hesitant feet. He'd lost the gun, so it was only them. Only strength.

They were a tangle of limbs fighting for their lives.

No. Valerie wasn't fighting for her life; she was fighting under orders. And that was the difference between them. She didn't have anything to lose. He did. He used every single tactic he had learned in the army, but also let his feelings help him. He let the adrenaline fuel him, the anger move his fists, the terror of losing Anna pumping through his muscles.

He managed to pin her down, and he let blow after blow fall to her face. He hated himself for hitting a woman, but he had to remember that this was not a woman. It was a soldier. A minion from the government. Valerie was almost unstoppable, her legs held onto his torso with incredible strength as she punched him right on the throat, choking him.

She twisted and got on top again. She had the advantage. His hands flew to her throat at the same time that hers flew to his. They both squeezed, and it was a battle of endurance he didn't know if he could win.

And then, there, in the corner of his eye, he saw Anna. She hadn't run.

Run, he thought.

She'd picked up his gun with trembling fingers and was aiming it at Valerie's head. She was right over Valerie's shoulder, her eyes on him. His vision was blurring, and he wanted to tell her so many things. That it was okay. That if she did it, she wasn't a bad person for it. He knew how hard the first kill was, knew by experience. His vision went dark, his hands slacking.

A gun was fired.

———

"Winston, Winston, please, wake up!"

The desperate plea woke something inside of Winston more than just his body and mind. It seemed to wake his soul.

"Anna…"

His eyes fluttered open, finding Anna lingering over him, her hands cradling his face on top of her lap. It was dark inside, but he could tell that her cheeks were tear stricken.

"Winston, are you okay? I thought, I thought…"

"Shh, shh, I'm okay. I'm okay."

His hands flew to her face, and she wiped the tears, now falling in earnest.

"Valerie?"

He tried to look around, but his head spun with the effort. He felt dizzy and tired.

"I think she's dead… I thought you were dead, too. You weren't waking up, and you lost so much blood. I'm so sorry. I'm sorry. I never… I never wanted to…"

Anna kept choking on her words as her tears dropped onto his chest, and Winston tried to understand what was going on through the fog in his mind. Blood? Why had he lost blood? He wasn't injured. It was just his head that hurt; it hurt so badly. That's when he noticed that only one of Anna's hands was cradling his face. The other was pressing hard against his shoulder.

"What happened? It's okay. I'm okay. I just need to know what happened."

Anna sucked in a deep breath and closed her eyes for a second before regaining her composure.

"I thought you were going to die. She was choking you, and I… I got the gun…"

"Yes, that was okay. You shot her, right?"

"I did, but the bullet… it…"

Anna looked down, and he followed her eyes, finding the spot that she was pressing on. His shoulder was bleeding heavily. The gun had small bullets —

bullets strong enough to break through armored vehi-cles. So, of course, it had gotten through Valerie's skull and came out the other side. Anna had saved him by shooting Valerie, but she had gotten him in the process, too.

"Anna, it's okay. Look at me." He guided her face to his with his good arm. "I'm okay, and you're okay. We'll be okay. Did you check Valerie's pulse?"

"No, but it's been minutes, and she's not moving. There's…" Anna gagged and covered her mouth.

"Shh, shh, it's okay. It's over, Anna. Look at me; it's over."

Anna's eyes found him again, and he did his best to smile up at her. He was injured, but he was sure he'd survive. He had a small first aid kit in his bag, and if they could bandage his shoulder, they could get out of there, take Valerie's van, and live. That was all that mattered now; he wanted for both of them to live.

"I need you to do one more thing for me, okay? I'm going to guide you through the process. But first of all, I need to know if there's an exit wound."

Anna nodded and slowly pulled him up, checking his back and nodding. He bit his tongue, not wanting her to know how much pain he was in.

"There's an exit wound," she said quietly.

"Then we're fine, Anna. We're fine. There's a first aid kit in my bag. I need you to get it and dress the wound for me. After that, we can get out of here, okay?"

"Yes, yes, I can do that… I can do that." Anna breathed deeply once more, and then gently lowered him to the floor. "I work in a lab, with blood all the time, you know? This is nothing new; I can do this."

"Of course, you can, love."

Anna chuckled and returned to his side with the kit, a soft smile on her face.

"That's the second time you called me that tonight. Did you know that?"

"Is it?" He felt a smile tugging at his lips, unable to hold it back. He hadn't even been aware of doing it, but he liked how it sounded. "I hope that's not an issue for you. I can stop doing it."

Anna chuckled again and threaded a needle with amble fingers. "I don't mind it, at all. But you might call me some other names once I'm done with this wound."

"Never."

Without much more to do, Winston bit the inside of his cheek as Anna started cleaning and sewing his wound. It had been a close call, but they were both alive. And they would make it. Even if it was the last thing he did with his life, he'd make sure Anna got out.

"Okay, here we go!"

Without waiting for an answer, Anna plunged the needle into his skin. But this time, it wasn't to get a fake blood sample; it was to save his life.

CHAPTER
THIRTEEN

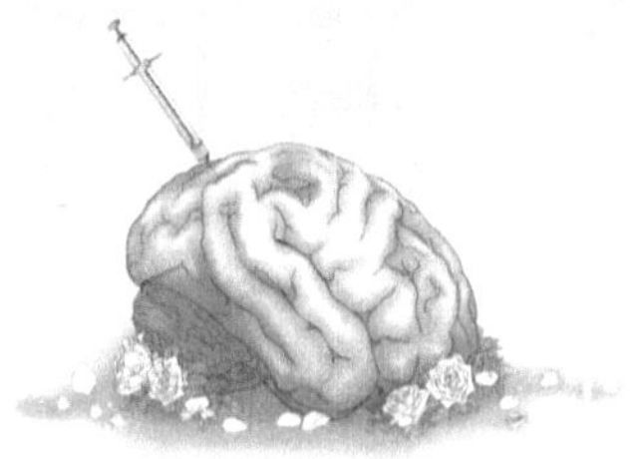

ANNA

"Are you sure you can stand?"

"Anna, I'm okay. I already said it five times; my legs are perfectly fine. You shot me in the shoulder, not the calf."

Anna scowled but couldn't stop a small laugh from bursting out of her lips. What a situation they were in!

She'd been terrified when she found out about Valerie, but seeing Winston struggle for his life had been worse.

She was going to run. She told herself that she was ready for it, that she was going to run, just the way he'd told her to. But she couldn't do it. Valerie was going to kill him, and the gun was there, just sitting there. And she'd done it. She had to.

"You did the right thing," Winston reminded her, running a hand down her cheek.

It was as if he could tell where her train of thought had taken her.

She had taken a life.

"It was her or us; you did the right thing," he repeated.

"I know, but that doesn't make it any easier."

She shook her head to stop the tears from falling. She didn't want to cry anymore; she wanted to move on, to get out of there. With an arm under his armpit, she helped Winston to his feet.

"I know it doesn't. But make sure to remind yourself that it was the right thing to do every time those thoughts come looking for you. Because they will. You will come back to this moment many times over the next few weeks, and maybe even months. Or years. Killing someone is not something you just forget about, but you learn to live with it. If it's them or you… I want it to always be you, okay?"

He held her face in a warm palm, and she pressed her cheek harder against it. Gently, Winston lifted his injured arm and placed it on her waist, moving his other hand to the back of her head and cradling her softly against his chest. The steady thrum of his heart-beat gave her hope.

He was okay. He was a strong soldier, made to endure battle, and a single bullet wasn't going to stop him. He was going to be okay; they were going to be okay.

"Thank you," she murmured against his warm chest. "Thank you for everything."

"For you, I'd do anything and more."

She glanced up, finding his kind eyes on her. She got lost in there for a moment, in the intensity of that simple gesture, in the warmth that a pair of eyes could radiate. In his embrace, she felt whole. For the first time in her life, she felt complete. Not because she had him, but because she had experienced love. Because she knew what it felt like to be terrified of losing someone, and that made her want to fight even more. She had one more reason to give this cause everything she had.

"Love… You know, how you used that word earlier?"

"Hmm?"

The hum traveled down his chest and vibrated against her cheek, against her whole body.

"I want you to know… I do, too."

"Do what?" It was almost a breathless question, his face already tilting down to be closer to her.

"Think of you as love."

She smiled, mirroring the expression that was taking over Winston's face.

"I love you, Anna."

"And I love you, too."

Softly, too scared to hurt him even more, she raised onto her toes and pressed a soft kiss to his lips. They had kissed before in the woods, but this, this was different. It was softer, gentler, full of love and care. It was a kiss that said how much they cared about each other, and how much they had already given for this. To be able to be together. To be able to return this kind of feeling to the rest of the world. Because if they could have this, then the world deserved to know about it and to have it, too.

"What's next?" asked Winston when they finally pulled apart.

"We head north. I don't have any better ideas than that. I don't know if anything that Valerie had said is true, but we can't go back. So, we will keep heading north and see if there's really a camp there. Maybe there are people the government hasn't managed to get to. And if not, we'll start over from there."

"I think you're right; that's the best we can do."

It was still late at night, but they had decided that they should be on the move. They couldn't stay there any longer and risk being caught. If Valerie didn't report soon, they were sure someone would go looking for them. So, they had to move, and they had to do it as fast as possible. They had already spent too much time healing Winston, probably a good half hour or more.

"Let's go."

With an arm around his waist, and Winston's arm over her shoulders, they walked out of the building together. The air outside was cold, but not as cold as the inside had been. And she still had Winston's jacket, so she was okay. They pressed on, step after step, slowly inching toward the van.

They were about halfway there when Winston tensed, his arm dropping from her shoulder.

"Is everything okay?" she asked.

"Shh… I think—"

Winston's words were cut short by a beam of light. Both their hands went to their faces on instinct. Clicking sounds came from all around them, and Anna's blood froze. Guns. It was the sound of guns.

"Raise your hands over your head, and do as you're told, or you'll be shot." The voice boomed through the forest, metallic and deprived of any emotion.

Her eyes adjusted enough to look around. There were Military vehicles surrounding them from all angles, bright lights pointed at them. And behind the lights: soldiers. Blackhats and, probably, Redwatchers too, all with guns aimed at them.

Anna looked at Winston's chest, at the red laser dot there. And then she looked up. She found his pleading eyes on her, regret plastered all over his face. And fear. So much fear.

"I'm so sorry, Anna. You should run…"

When the words left his lips, Winston lunged toward the army in a sprint.

CHAPTER
FOURTEEN

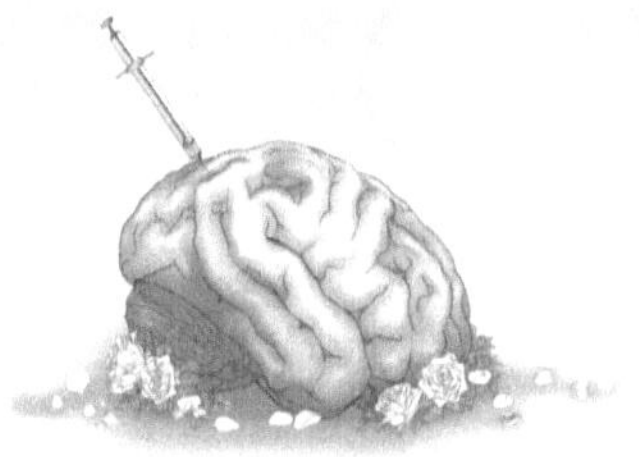

WINSTON

His mind was almost blank as he raced toward the army in front of them. There was only one thing that mattered: giving Anna a chance to run. He knew it was slim, he knew it was almost impossible, but he hoped that having all the attention on him would give her the small chance she needed.

It was all so fast. Barely seconds.

He ran, his feet kicking up dirt. Anna screamed his name. The closest soldier shot a dart into his bad shoulder. The electric shock sent him to the ground.

"Winston!"

He wanted to turn, to look at her, to tell her that she should be running. But his entire body was convulsing on the ground, the mixture of a potent electric shock and a mild sedative already taking hold of his body. He knew those weapons too well, and knew that he was done for.

Knowing was probably the worst of it, because it took his hope away. They had nothing. Nothing else to do, nothing else to fight for.

Anna was by his side in a second, her hands cupping his face, tears splashing on his torso.

"I… told you… to run," he managed to gasp out.

"And you're an idiot if you thought I would leave you."

The loud thump of boots intensified, and Anna was yanked away from him. He tried to scream, his throat raw and unwilling. They had her handcuffed in a second, her legs kicking, her eyes fixed on him.

It was the most horrible thing he'd ever seen. Her scared eyes, her thrashing limbs, the too-rough hands holding onto her upper arms and probably leaving bruises there.

He felt the little hope he had leaving his body and shattering against the ground.

Tears streamed down his cheeks as a soldier flipped him onto his back and handcuffed him, too. His eyes never left Anna, never. They took her onto a van, shoved her in the back. They got him on his feet, and he took a step toward Anna, not caring about the handcuffs, the unbearable pain in his shoulder, anything.

"And where do you think you're going, Romeo?" the soldier asked nonchalantly into his ear.

He was shoved back, his body twisting in peculiar angles as he tried to keep his eyes on Anna. They were taking him to a separate van.

"No, no. Take me with her, take me with her!"

He tried to squirm out of the soldier's hold, only to have a finger shoved into his bullet wound. He doubled over and was pushed onto his knees again.

"Cooperate, or you'll get worse than that."

No, no, no. It couldn't be happening. It couldn't! He looked over his shoulder, just before the doors of the van closed, and Anna was shoved out of his life.

"Anna…"

"Move, soldier."

He was lifted back onto his feet and pushed toward an empty van. Winston didn't know what else to do.

What's the point in fighting anymore? We'd tried it all and failed.

As he was thrown into the back of the van and the door closed, he closed with it. He pushed it all in, deep down, as he had done when he was a kid.

There was no more hope, no reason to keep going.

CHAPTER
FIFTEEN

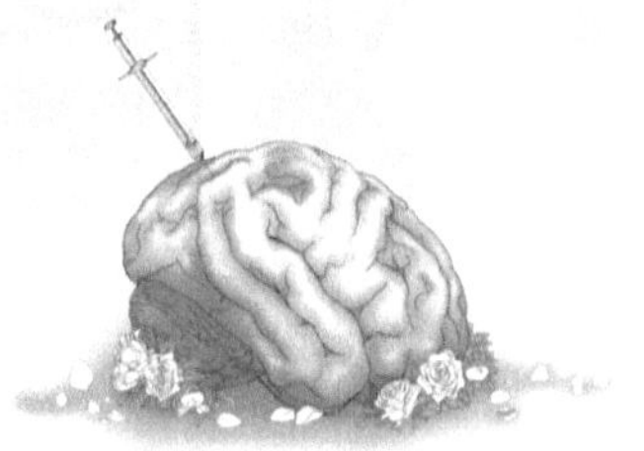

ANNA

As the door to the van closed, and Winston's eyes were taken away from her sight, Anna screamed. She had fought with tooth and nail trying to get away from the Redwatchers and the Blackhats, and her fingers were bloody and sore, her cheeks covered with tears. But none of it mattered. They had gotten so close. They knew they weren't the only ones, and that the government was indeed eliminating people with emotions.

She was aware that was probably her destiny. She'd be taken into a prison, probably be given a sort of deadly serum that would wipe her out for good. Her records would disappear from the public eye, and it'd be like she'd never existed. Anna's parents would be told to never speak her of name again or risk death. And they would agree, because they didn't care. They couldn't care. She'd become another file with a red aberration stamp on it.

The van started up, and the gravel under the wheels marked the movement of time for the next hour while she was taken back into the city. There was no other place they could take her to, so she knew that'd be it. She'd never heard of prisoners before, so she wondered where they were taking her. She wondered where they were taking Winston, too. Probably back to the Military, where they'd attempt to brainwash him or hang him on the spot.

It was painful to know so much about how Faulkner dealt with things and be able to anticipate his moves. It pained her. With her hands tightly bound behind her back, Anna used her shoulder to wipe away the tears.

Those would be the last of them.

She wouldn't cry anymore, wouldn't allow them to see her weaknesses. She was strong, and she could make it. She was going to make it. Finding a way out was her first priority, so she started looking around the van, hoping for any small thing she could use to her advantage.

But there was nothing.

Too fast, the van stopped. It was getting bright outside, and when the doors opened, she was almost blinded by the first morning rays.

"Get down."

The male soldier pointed to the ground, and Anna obeyed. She was going to get out, but she also needed to know which battles to pick. An armed soldier wasn't the one.

She jumped down and looked around. A tall building was to the front, a big parking lot all around it. Weeds were growing between the paving stones, the place clearly abandoned. The yellowish walls of the building had pieces of paint falling off, and some windows were broken and boarded.

As they walked closer to the building, two soldiers flanking her, a sign came into view.

Bellevue Psychiatric Hospital.

Her blood chilled, and her bones ached, at the sight of it. Anna knew the place. Hell, everyone knew that place. It was where everything had started, where Faulkner's reign had grown from nothing, and where the first Siero serum had been created. Where hundreds of patients had been vaccinated and later committed suicide.

She was taken inside through a side door protected by a code and accessed with a magnetic card. Inside, the place seemed deserted. They walked down a hall and there: another human. A woman with a medical coat was standing in a small room, a syringe in her hand. Anna squirmed, trying to get away from her, but the woman approached in silence and — with the help of the soldiers — took her jacket off and plunged the needle into Anna's upper arm.

Her vision went blurry in an instant, and the only thing she could think of was the jacket the nurse now held in her hands. Winston's jacket.

Don't take it, she wanted to say, but the words failed her as the world turned pitch black.

———

When she woke up, the room she was in was almost dark. A small lightbulb flickered on the ceiling. A little confused, she looked around. The metal frame of the bed squeaked as she tried to sit down and found that she couldn't move. A little desperation clawed inside her throat, and she pushed up, but nothing happened. Both of Anna's wrists were restrained with thick leather straps, and she could barely lift her chest enough to look around the room — a room that was more like a prison cell.

There was nothing but a chair and a doorless closet to one side, which was empty. A small glass window was high up on the wall, barely a shred of light coming through it. The mattress she was on was thin, and she could feel the metal underneath, each plank digging into her back. She was wearing a thin medical robe, Winston's jacket nowhere to be seen.

Panic made her heart race, and Anna did her best to breathe deeply through her nose. In and out. In and out. When calmness finally took over her, she was left in silence, her breathing and the ticking of a clock behind her back the only thing breaking the stillness.

She couldn't turn enough to see the time, only heard its incessant ticking.

Tick. Tick. Tick. Each second felt like a lifetime.

Where is Winston? Is he even alive? Why haven't they killed me yet? How can I get out? I need to get out.

Tick. Tick. Tick.

Minutes passed, and no one came. So, Anna screamed at the top of her lungs. Screamed for someone to come and help her. For someone to tell her what was going on. For food. For someone to let her go to the bathroom. She screamed until her throat was raw.

Tick. Tick. Tick.

She screamed in anger, in frustration, in pain, and in fear. But she didn't let a single tear roll down. She wouldn't let them see her cry again.

When nothing happened, and her voice started to fail her, Anna closed her eyes. She saw Winston there, his short hair and fearful eyes. His lustful eyes. His hopeful eyes. She saw Winston, his face contorted in pain as he was taken away from her — their last memory together. Anna snapped her eyes open and stared at the small window, seeing how the light dimmed in slow motion.

She couldn't think like that. Couldn't let fear and pain rule her. She was smart; she would figure something out.

CHAPTER
SIXTEEN

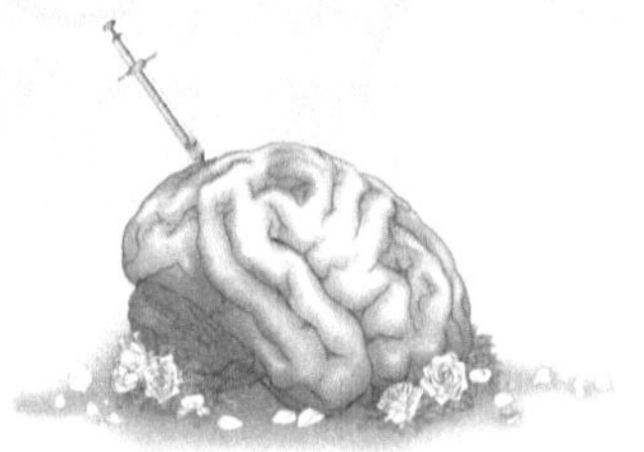

WINSTON

Expecting to be taken straight into the woods to be hung or shot, Winston was surprised when the van rolled to a stop, and he was let out to find a familiar camp. *His* Military camp.

Instead of heading to the barracks, he was taken to

one of the furthest buildings… the ones where only the highest-ranking soldiers were allowed. He was taken in shackles, his head hanging low, his soul hanging in tatters. Halls merged one into the other as he was taken further into the heart of the building, away from the outside world, away from the comfort he had learned to find in his barracks.

A few floors down, and too many halls to recall where he was, Winston stood in front of a thick metal door.

He was thrown inside the cell; the door closed behind him.

And then, darkness was his only company. Darkness and despair.

ANNA

Time was a curious thing. A curious and twisted thing. Had it been days? Hours? Weeks? Silence was everything she had. Silence, and the dreaded ticking of that damn clock. She wished she could rip it down. Hit it with a hammer. Slam it against a wall.

Food was delivered at irregular intervals, time such a slippery thing that she couldn't understand it anymore. Anna was so tired. Just so tired. She had fought against the restraints, her wrists raw, her head pounding with the echo of her own screams. But nothing had worked. They hadn't let her go. She was sure that days had passed, maybe even a week. Or a month. Time was so curious, just so curious.

The familiar loud click of the lock sounded, but she didn't even turn.

What's the point?

They'd give her some food, and then be gone. She hoped it was the chicken flavor thing, not the other disgusting mixture they usually gave her. Maybe they'd give her another shot, monitor her vitals as her body seized and convulsed. She wondered what kind of concoctions they were trying out on her, and if they were attempting to erase her emotions once more.

She had become a lab rat.

The large nurse's shadow loomed over her, but still, Anna didn't look. She told herself she was waiting for the right moment, for a flicker of hope so she could escape. But the truth was that she was losing whatever hope she'd had.

She had asked to speak with someone, to be let out, to be able to talk to her parents, Faulkner, a Blackhat, anyone. But none of her questions had been answered. All they did was give her different serums, some food when she was lucky, and then leave her alone once more.

Is this what the first subjects felt like? Like they were losing their minds?

She wasn't sure if her emotions were duller, or if there was nothing to be felt among those four walls. Her mind… her mind was the last thing she'd lose. She pictured Winston, his hopeful eyes, his scared ones. The scared ones were the ones that came to her more often than not those days.

She seemed unable to forget about the look on his face just before the van's doors closed between them. The last time she had seen him.

Would it be the last?

No. She couldn't think like that. She had to find a way out, a way to fight… but she didn't even know if Winston was still alive.

————

WINSTON

Trying to count the passing of days had been fruitless. Winston wasn't sure what was real and what was not anymore, his face too bruised to even open his eyes properly, his body an aching mess.

The physical torture wasn't even the worse, no. He knew physical pain, and it was easy enough to deal with. The hard part had been the live videos they made him watch: Anna's almost expressionless face, the fight leaving her body.

At first, he had seen her struggle against her restraints, scream, fight. But now… now she was simply there, her body almost limp. The image was a little grainy and in shades of gray, and he thought that was so fitting.

Their lives were a dull shade of gray now. They never let her out of that bed, and he watched how they pierced their skin with needles over and over.

He couldn't help her.

Every time he was kicked on the ribs, he was asked if he was ready to forget about her, to rejoin the force. Every time, he said her name.

"Anna."

It was a plea for them to stop; it was a last wish to see her once more, to touch her, to feel her.

"Anna."

It was a desperate attempt to get those ruthless soldiers to feel something. To snap out of their expressionless lives, to feel a tinge of what he was feeling.

"Anna."

It was the only thing that had mattered. It had been the hope that a different life was possible, that he could have more than he had ever wished for.

But as the days passed, it was harder and harder to even say her name.

What's the point? What am I even fighting for?

ANNA

"Rise and shine," a bored voice said as the door opened once more.

Unfamiliar to words lately, Anna jumped, a little startled.

The nurse went to her side and, to Anna's surprise, started unlatching her restraints.

Is this it? Is this my chance to get out?

She tried not to move, not to react. She had to wait for the perfect time, that had been the plan, right?

After loosening both restraints a little, the nurse gave her one more shot, and then completely undid the leather straps before quickly leaving the room and locking the door. She had left the used syringe on the small side table, and Anna couldn't believe her eyes as she grabbed it. Her eyes darted around the room once more. Nothing had changed... Nothing but the jacket that had shown up, hanging on the back of the metal chair while she slept.

"Winston..."

She stood up on trembling legs, her muscles so sore that it felt like pins and needles stabbed at the sole of her bare feet as she made her way toward the Military jacket — the syringe still tightly clutched in between her fingers.

Anna barely made it there, walking the short steps that separated her from the jacket being the hardest thing she'd ever done. Her legs gave out, and she slid against the wall, all the way to the floor as she tried to find any remnants of Winston's earthy scent on the jacket — but there was nothing. Nothing there.

A gentle click of metal against the floor made her look down at the syringe she had dropped — the only weapon she had. Her only way out. She could inject air into the nurse and make a run for it. It was the only way. She picked it up again and saw the name of the drug on a small label on the plastic tube.

Siero — prototype I.

5 ml.

Her blood chilled, and her bones seemed to ache.

"No, no, no…"

————

WINSTON

A hard fist collided with his cheek, and Winston tasted the blood coating the inside of his mouth. It was the flavor he was most used to by then.

"Are you ready to rejoin the force?"

Silence.

A kick to his stomach as he tried to curl up on the floor and protect his internal organs.

"Soldier Hitcher, are you ready to plead allegiance to Bellevue and Faulkner, and rejoin the force?"

Winston's lips parted.

"A…"

Can I even say it? Can I even say her name again?

He hadn't seen any videos in what felt like weeks, and he didn't even know if Anna was still alive. Any small shred of hope he had of seeing her again was leaving his body, along with the blood pouring out of the corner of his mouth.

He swallowed and curled his arms, holding onto his knees, his head resting on the cold floor.

"Make… it… stop."

The soldier's leg stopped halfway to his face. Winston waited for another blow but, a moment later, the door to his cell closed with the familiar click of a lock, and he was left in darkness again.

———

ANNA

"Why?" she asked the empty room. "Why now?"

Anna wondered what had changed. Had they broken Winston and gotten him to speak? Was he dead? Had they decided that she wasn't useful anymore? She knew what Prototype I was like. She knew it had been the one to wipe out emotions so badly that the side effects had led hundreds of people to kill themselves.

"I will never do it," she chanted to herself. "I will never give them that satisfaction."

But wouldn't it be better? A voice asked inside her head.

If she was going to die, she would rather do it by her own hands than wait for the scientists and government to kill her. *Right?*

Anna clutched Winston's jacket as hard as she could, trying to remember every little moment when she was by his side. The feel of his fingers on her face, of his hands wrapping around her waist, of his lips pressing on hers. It was hard to do, but she had to. She had to believe that she had the strength to remember it, to feel it.

How long had it been since they'd given her the shot? She'd been unable to stand from her spot against the wall, but she thought days might have passed again. Time seemed to pass so slow and so fast all at once. She could see the clock on the opposite wall now,

but its hands were stuck on three and two —
unmoving.

With her head pressed against the cold wall, Anna breathed slowly, trying to stay present. Her fingers found a few lines on the wall, as if someone had been counting days in there. She started counting them, but got lost somewhere around seventy-eight, or maybe ninety-eight. The marks were small and jagged, as if scratched with a nail or something that wasn't too sharp.

Anna's nails were long after being there for so long, so she slowly moved her index finger up and down until she added one more line to the count. The days didn't matter, but she wanted to leave a little something to show that she'd been there.

More marks appeared on the spot where she was leaning against the wall, so she pushed back and sat with her legs crossed, looking at the wall.

And there, under more and more lines… something different. Curved and small lines made with careful precision gave her a name: Constance.

Someone named Constance had spent days and nights in the same cell, just as she was doing. Anna picked up the syringe again, and with the sharp end, scribbled her name underneath it.

Constance.

Anna.

———

WINSTON

"Soldier Hitcher," an emotionless voice said as the door to his cell opened once more.

Winston braced for the torture, for a kick to his ribs, but nothing happened.

"Stand up. You're being taken to see the general."

Winston stood up, and the light outside was almost blinding when the soldier put a hand on his shoulder to usher him forward. A second soldier was waiting outside the door, and as he walked with his head hanging low, a flicker of something he knew caught his eye.

He looked up, "John?" The soldier didn't even flinch, so he asked again, "Mad Dog?"

His bunkmate barely glanced at him and kept walking, taking him over to see the general.

Winston didn't know what he was in for, but all fight had left him already.

How much worse can it get?

CHAPTER
SEVENTEEN

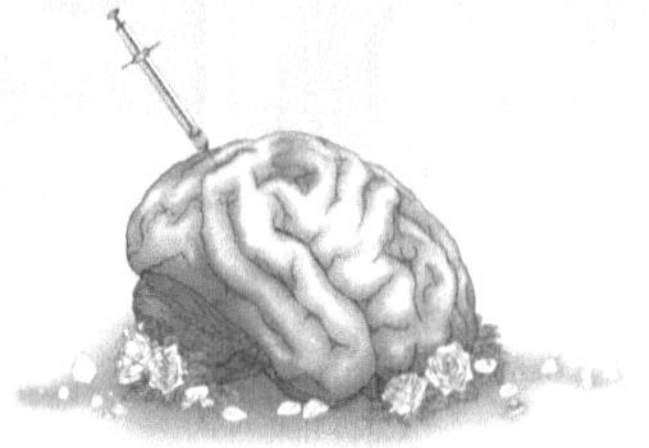

ANNA

The next time the clicking of keys sounded on the other side of the thick metal door, Anna was ready. She didn't have much left to fight for, didn't remember what it felt like to be held in between Winston's arms, but she knew that the small room wouldn't be the last place to hold her. She knew the jacket she was wearing belonged to someone she'd cared about, even if she couldn't make herself feel like she cared anymore. Thinking of Winston was like thinking about the broken clock on the wall — she felt nothing.

Instead of waiting for the nurse by her bed, she quietly dragged herself behind the door and stood with her back against the wall. She'd never seen anyone other than the same nurse who came in every day, so it should be easy enough. It should be.

Her breathing was steady, and her heart was beating consistently as Anna waited. Her head was clear — she knew exactly what she had to do. She might not have felt a thing, but that didn't mean that she was willing to die in that room alone.

If there was something she was sure of, it was that old Anna would have wanted her to do this. To get out. To see the world one last time in hopes of feeling a little something.

The door opened an inch, two. She heard one step. Anna pushed the entire weight of her body against the door as fast as she could and heard the nurse groan. She loosened the piece of metal that had been keeping her locked for so long as fast as her legs would take her.

The nurse was on the floor, clutching her bleeding forehead. There was no time to worry about her, so Anna ran. She ran like she would've run if her life depended on it. Did it? Maybe it did, but Anna couldn't care about it. She ran for old Anna, for the memories of what she'd been, for the feelings she couldn't remember.

WINSTON

"Soldier Hitcher, I hear you're ready to negotiate your return to the force," the general said as he sat in front of him.

Winston didn't say a word, too stunned to think straight.

Is that what they thought? That I'm ready to return? Am I?

"We're offering you your old place back. You'll be graduating in two months, and when you do, we'll recommend you for deployment. You'll be taken onto the front lines like you've always envisioned. All you need to do is commit to your old schedule. Forget about the woman."

The woman.

Anna.

"Anna…."

The general nodded, and the soldier standing behind him placed a screen on the desk that separated him from his superior. He turned on the screen, and images from a security camera showed up. It wasn't the room he was used to, but a hallway. And in the middle of it: Anna. She was running and about to turn a corner. But she couldn't see what he saw: a guard posed at the end of the hall that she was about to turn into.

Winston's heart hammered in his chest, cold sweat gathering in the back of his neck. He kept his face expressionless as he watched, nausea creeping up his throat, fingers clutching the edge of the desk as hard as he could.

Anna.

ANNA

Anna turned a corner and skidded to a stop. A few feet ahead, a soldier stood against the door that she thought would take her outside. He pointed the gun at her, his eyes invisible behind the shield of his helmet. Anna lifted her hands slowly as her eyes scanned her surroundings. Then she darted to the left and took the stairs, two at a time.

She didn't know the building, but if out wasn't an option, she'd at least go up. So, up she went. Up and up and up, heading toward the stars that had been her only company for so many lonely nights.

She could almost remember what loneliness had felt like. She could taste it on her tongue, but even though she knew that she should be feeling lonely in the middle of nowhere, left alone to rot, she couldn't. She didn't.

So, Anna kept running up as fast as her legs would take her. One floor, then two, then three. The sound of boots heavy against the steps followed, but she didn't slow down. They yelled for her to stop, yelled for her to surrender.

Surrender? What do they know about surrendering?

Anna had already surrendered everything she had

and everything she was. There was nothing left. Nothing but the stars high up in the sky, waiting for her to join them.

WINSTON

His heart was wild in his chest as the image on the screen changed from a security camera to a Military one. He knew those too well. They were small cameras placed on soldiers' helmets so they could report directly to the base and have their generals know what was happening.

And now, he was watching Anna's back through that soldier's camera, her small figure disappearing behind the turn of the stairs over and over again, and reappearing once more.

What's she doing? Why's she going up? There's no way out up there!

"This ends today, soldier. You have to make a choice. Who do you stand with? That woman, or us?"

Anna was out of screen once more, and a second later, the soldier reached an exit door — a door to the rooftop. It was half-open, and the soldier pushed it, stepping into the moonlit night.

ANNA

She hadn't known that it was nighttime before stepping onto the roof, but she had almost felt it inside, like a knowledge she simply possessed. The stars were glistening all around her, and she tried to recall what it had felt like to be so small, to have the world in front of her. But she couldn't.

She walked over to the edge of the roof, stood on the ledge, and looked up. Then down. Trees stretched far beyond, and the ground seemed to be so far away.

How many levels had I climbed? How far up am I?

She didn't know, but she didn't think it mattered anymore. The night had seeped into her; it had taken over her heart and turned it into a black pit.

Or is that the serum?

"Anna Chaplin, step off the ledge, and turn around with your hands up."

She wanted to laugh but couldn't remember how to. So, she turned.

The soldier who faced her had his gun pointed at her, the red dot like a small firefly dancing over her chest.

"I will not shoot you unless you make me," the soldier said in a bored tone. "I have orders to return you to your room if you cooperate."

"And spend the rest of my days in a closed room? I have lived all there is to live, but I can't remember what any of it feels like."

Anna opened her arms wide and took a step back, her heels tasting emptiness as she almost toppled back into the abyss behind her.

"I'm sorry, Winston," she said out loud, hoping that

he was already with the stars and listening to her. She looked up and drew a smile on her face, the muscles used to the movement even if her heart wasn't anymore. "I think I love you."

———

WINSTON

His fingers hurt where he clutched the edge of the desk as hard as he could. He thought he'd splinter the wood as he watched Anna standing on the ledge. She opened her arms wide, and her lips moved, a soft smile on her face — but there was no audio on the video.

"She'd been given the chance to surrender," the general said.

Winston barely heard him over the roaring of his own heart.

And then Anna fell back.

CHAPTER
EIGHTEEN

WINSTON

An official entered the barracks and woke them up. The soldiers jumped from their bunks, Mad Dog landing on the floor with a loud thump.

"It's a six-mile run today," John said as if reminding himself of the fact.

Winston barely nodded, got ready, and together, they got out of the barracks and onto the track. They ran side by side as they had done so many times before. They ran side by side, as if the last two months of their lives hadn't even happened. Like nothing had changed.

But everything was different.

Winston had found someone like him. He'd learned that love was possible. He had given his heart and soul. And then, both of those had been ripped from his chest. He'd been tortured and made to watch the woman he loved fall to her death. The grainy image of Anna's sprawled body in the distance, recorded from the soldier's camera, was ingrained in his mind.

"Nothing left to lose, soldier," the general had said. "Are you with us?"

He couldn't remember replying, but he must have.

The next day, he had woken back in his cot, his body drenched in cold sweat from the nightmares that now clouded his every night.

Failing Anna wasn't even the worst of it.

But what do I have left?

At least this way, he'd be deployed and leave this place. If he were lucky, he'd be sent to the front lines and be shot in the head, so he wouldn't have to think about her anymore. It was too painful to do so.

So, Winston ran because he had nothing left to do. He ran, and he showered. He fought, and he patrolled. He practiced his aim with a gun and spent his nights surrounded by those he blamed for Anna's death.

———

It was his third week back when he returned to the labs for the usual shot. He hadn't been getting any because the generals knew he didn't need them, but they wanted him to be more reactive — so he was back in the dreaded place where he had met her.

Winston fought hard to keep his expression neutral as he swiped his card and walked in. The white walls of the halls made the place look so big, but there was not enough air inside. The hallway stretched forever until he found the door he was looking for. He walked in, found the usual nurse, and was injected with the shot in barely seconds. It was all the same as usual, but Winston couldn't help but look for a tinge of copper hair in every corner.

But, of course, he didn't find her.

Instead, when he was almost out, he heard someone murmuring his name. "Winston?"

He turned around and found a familiar girl standing beside him. She had dark braids, down to her waist, and equally dark eyes that looked right into him.

"Sammy?" Winston remembered the girl that he'd seen in Anna's lab, and the connection to her almost broke him.

Sammy quickly ran to his side and almost bumped into him. Her fingers twitched at her sides, and her pupils were dilated, making her eyes look almost black.

"Sorry," she whispered as she placed a hand against his chest to steady herself. "I need to watch where I'm going. Just wanted to say hi." Her tone was loud enough for the few people around to hear them.

Sammy looked around to those lingering about, but

no one was paying them much attention. She looked a little nervous as she leaned in closer and whispered against his shoulder.

"Anna wanted you to have this if anything happened to her."

With that, the girl turned around and disappeared between the workers coming and going. Winston felt the piece of paper the girl had smuggled into his pocket, and he dug his hands in them, pushing it to the bottom and walking out of the Fox Lab as if nothing had happened.

———

Winston had been too scared to look at the paper in front of anyone, so he had ignored it for almost two days before he finally got the weekend off and claimed that he had to go drop some supplies off at his family's home. It wasn't unusual for soldiers to take provisions to their families, so no one questioned him when he signed his leave for the day.

Taking one of the Military vehicles, he made his way to the suburbs. He walked the familiar streets to the unmarked door and knocked.

It was only a minute until a plump woman opened it. "Winston, come on in."

"How's everything going, Mother?"

"Same as usual. Everybody's working, so I'm home alone. I can get you some food if you're hungry."

Sara barely looked at him as she went into the kitchen and kept working on what she was doing.

"That'd actually be perfect, Mother. Thanks. I will be in my old room for a moment and would appreciate not being disturbed."

"Of course." Sara waved a hand his way and kept stirring a pot of something that smelled like rabbit stew.

Winston crossed the small hall to the room that had been his when he was younger. Before that, the house had belonged to their grandparents, and Winston knew it would've been his grandma's.

He was about twelve years old when he'd found the secret compartment under a loose floorboard, where his grandmother kept her journals, and he'd never told anyone about it. His grandma, Cady, had talked about emotions, about things Winston understood but knew he couldn't talk about, so he had felt a strong connection to them from the start and made sure to keep them a secret from the rest of the world — even his own family.

Back in his childhood room after so long, memories assaulted him, but he tried not to let them get to him. He closed the door and locked it before sitting on the single bed that now resided in the room in case anyone ever stayed the night. He fished the piece of paper from his pocket and stared at the folded note.

When had she written it? It had to be from before we fled if Sammy had it, but why? Had she known something could go wrong?

He rubbed his fingers on the edge of the paper a few times before gathering enough courage to open it up.

As soon as he unfolded it though, he had to blink away tears in order to see the words scribbled there.

The image of Anna falling backwards played in his mind over and over again, so he shook his head. This was everything he had left of her; he had to be strong. Slowly, he read the words.

Winston, if this gets to you, it's because things haven't gone as we planned. I know I'm making a hot-headed decision by choosing to trust Valerie and follow her to who-knows-where, but I have to take the chance. My whole life, I've been waiting for chances like this. I never knew anyone like me, with enough feelings to know what it meant to be me.

But then you showed up. You showed up in that lab like you were a God-sent, and that comes from someone who doesn't even believe in a god. But seeing you there, I had to believe in something.

I've been working on something for a very long time since the first day I stepped into the Fox Lab. It had been my Plan A for a long time, but when you showed up, I had to give Plan B a go. I had to risk it all for you... How could I not? The way you look at me and hold me in your arms make me believe in the possibility of a better world. A world where people can be like you and me, where there can be love, hope, and beautiful memories being created every day.

We're living like empty carcasses, being led by other people's choices, but we can't keep going like this. There was a world before us that was better. A world where people could love as you and I can. And I want to give that back to the world, to Bellevue. I don't know if things outside the wall are the same as here, but I choose to believe that they are not. I have to believe that, by returning the emotions to Bellevue, I will be doing what's right.

But Winston, if this gets to you, it's because something

went wrong. It means that I'm not around anymore, but for some reason, you are. Winston… I love you. I love you like I never knew I could love another human. I love you so much it hurts. It hurts to know that so many people are deprived of what we have. We have to give it back. We have to allow people to feel this.

So, if this flimsy piece of paper is between your hands, I have one favor to ask. You have to take over my Plan A.

Winston took a deep breath and wiped the tears streaming down his cheeks before he finished reading Anna's plan. And then he read the whole thing again. And again.

"I love you," he whispered, knowing that she'd never hear those words again.

Even though he had things to do and places to be, Winston allowed himself a moment with Anna's letter. He read it so many times that he had almost memorized it by the time he stooped onto the floor and got the loose floorboard out.

He took his grandma's journals out from the inside and looked through them one more time. As a kid, he'd looked at them with fear. He'd checked a few pages here and there, read his grandma's stories about love and death, and then put them away, fearing that someone would find him with the diaries in his hands.

Now, having almost nothing left to lose, he opened them up and marveled at them slowly.

He read the first few pages, where his grandmother talked about a love so great that it had driven her mad when she lost it. He read about the short years Cadence had spent in a mental health clinic while her sister looked after her child because she was unable to be a good enough mother to Sara.

"Bellevue is a tricky and treacherous place," Cady had written. "There are needles that pierce, but others that soothe. There are people who stare, but others who listen. Walls that listen. Lights that blind. Trees that whisper."

From what he'd gathered, his grandma, Cady, had been at Bellevue when the first Siero serum had been created. She had been released and was allowed to go back home, where she had written most of her diaries. But her time had been cut short. Her handwriting had gotten neat and almost perfect, but then it had gotten messy all over again. She had written loose phrases here and there that scared twelve-year-old Winston.

"No one is safe."

"They'd doomed us all."

"People are dying everywhere. Everywhere. My friends are dead. The ones I loved are dead. The ones I hated are dead. They're all dead."

The last pages were plagued with cuttings from local newspapers. A note about a woman who had jumped from a roof. Another who had taken enough sleeping pills to kill an army. A man who had jumped in front of a moving vehicle.

That one had a small note on the side that said, "I remember him."

Winston read the entire article, which described the death of Kai Hastings, a man who had been a scientist at the psychiatric hospital but had later been a patient after some unconfirmed diagnosis of mental illness. He had been a patient at the same time as his grandma had been, and Winston wondered if they'd been friends. The man had simply jumped in front of a moving vehicle, taking his own life.

The last note was one from a woman named Constance Fay. There was only a note by its side that said, "I'll join you soon, Connie." Winston had been too scared to ever ask how his grandmother had lost her life, but after reading so many articles, he knew suicide had been the cause of it. Almost four hundred lives had been lost that year to the first Siero, but it was something almost no one talked about. Winston put everything away and read Anna's letter one last time.

He knew what he had to do.

CHAPTER
NINETEEN

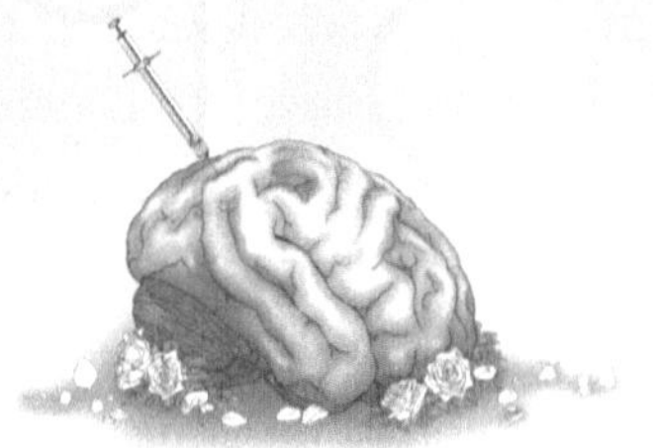

WINSTON

Before leaving the house, Winston planted a kiss on his mother's forehead. Sara looked at him as if he had just done the strangest thing in the world, but he simply walked off. He had no time for emergency good-byes. If he was going to do it, he had to do it before he changed his mind. Before he chickened out, or someone found out about the note.

Just like Anna had done a few weeks back, he was making a hot-headed decision. He was throwing everything in. He jumped back onto the Military van and drove over to the alley, where he'd always met with Anna. She'd told him in her letter that he was going to find the rest of the plan and what he needed in the place where they had kissed for the first time. It was coded to make sure only Winston would find what Anna had been working on, and he felt a surge of emotion in his chest that he couldn't give a name to.

Maybe it was pride. Pride that she had chosen him for the task, that she had believed in him in a way he hadn't even believed in himself. If it wasn't for Anna, he would've never considered leaving the army in the first place. He would've never considered ditching the only place he had ever known as a home. His barracks, his bunkmates. But he couldn't even call them his friends. And Anna? He had called her his love. Winston had known with her something he hadn't known existed otherwise. And now, she was asking him to do one last thing for her, for all of Bellevue. And in her memory, he'd do everything in his power to make it a reality.

He'd give the town their emotions back.

The alley was deserted, and the sound of his steps resonated in the emptiness as he ran toward the forest. No one paid him much attention, but he looked both ways before entering the edge of the forest, in case anyone was following him. But no one was.

The clearing opened up in front of him within a few minutes, and Winston dashed over to the tree that they had leaned against. The one where Anna had laid a blanket for them to eat grapes and berries together. The one where he knew Anna had hidden what he was looking for. He walked around the trunk, looking for any marks, until he found a small hole in the bark.

Inside, was a small plastic bag with a note. He ripped the plastic and unfolded the piece of paper. The same handwriting as before greeted him, and Winston read Anna's plan. Read how she'd trusted Sammy because she was the only emotionless human she had met who was smart enough to understand that life with emotions would've been better.

Anna had given her vials of emotions as often as she could, so Sammy could understand what Anna was talking about. The only other person besides Winston that she had trusted with her secret. And the one she had gone to before leaving with Valerie, in case anything went wrong.

Anna had told Sammy to give Winston the first note at the first chance she got if Anna didn't return. In that first note, he had been told to return to the forest and look for the next clue. And now, he sat under the well-known tree and read the words of his lover one more time.

Follow the map until you find what I've been working on.

So, not having any better plan than to listen to her, Winston followed the map of the forest toward a stream.

It was a half-hour hike that led Winston to a frigid stream. The water was almost freezing cold to the touch, and Winston knew immediately why Anna had left her investigation there. She needed the serum that she had created to stay cold for as long as possible in case she couldn't return to it for a long time. In case anything failed.

And it had.

According to her first letter, Anna had been working on a cure for years. Knowing that the chances of administering it to humans as a shot was slim, she had worked on a new formula that could be drank like cough medicine. Before leaving, she had tried the serum on Sammy, who Anna claimed had regained her emotions after a few short days.

The formula was now a concentrated version that Anna had planned on releasing to the waterways so that it would get to the entire city. It wasn't the best plan, but Anna had known that it was the best she could do without a bigger team of people supporting them. After all, they were alone.

Winston dug between the rocks that Anna had marked with a red cross, and started piling them by the side of the stream, his fingers going numb after a few minutes. When he was done, he found a small cooler that had been hiding in plain sight. He took it out and opened it. Inside, one last note waited for him, along with two glass vials.

Winston, I'm leaving you with my legacy. With everything I've ever worked on. With this note, is a map of the water purification plant and the entry points that you can use to sneak in. Once inside, find the purified tanks and drop the contents of one of the vials into it. If you find the chemical tanks, you can drop the contents there, instead.

Keep the second one so other investigators can replicate my work once the town has their emotions back. If this has spread to other cities as we've been led to believe, they'll need this to produce more and help others, too. Thank you for this. Thank you for everything. If you're reading this, and I'm gone, I want you to know that I don't regret any of it. I chose the life I chose, and I chose to allow myself to love you. And I would do it a thousand times over if I could.

Live for me, Winston. Live for us. Make this world better. With love, Anna.

"I will. I promise, I will."

Pocketing both vials, Winston returned to his van. The water purification plant was on the edge of the city limits, just inside the wall, so he made his way there without delay.

———

He'd been a soldier. A lover. A fool. But above all, he knew he had his training to rely on. So, Winston steadied his own heart as he jumped over the fence and snuck inside the plant. The building didn't have much security, as there was no point in guarding a place like it, so immobilizing the guard at the back entrance had been simple enough.

Winston was a soldier, a human madly in love, and a fool. Because of his haste to do what Anna had asked of him, Winston forgot the basic running of the Military. He forgot what those people were capable of. So, when he found his way to the tank, and a group of ten armed soldiers pointed their guns at him, he knew he'd messed up.

"Soldier Hitcher, put your hands up, and step away from the water tank."

Winston's heart dropped to the ground at the sound of Mad Dog's voice.

Why him? Why'd they have to send him?

He'd only been inside the building for a few minutes before the armed forces barged in. He had been a fool, such a fool. And now, he was going to die because of it. One act of treason, the army could deal with, but him going rogue twice? He knew he wouldn't leave the building in one piece.

"You've been tracking me, haven't you?" he asked, trying to win a little bit of time.

The vial in his right hand felt sweaty, and he held onto it harder so as to not drop it.

"Yes, Hitcher, we have. Your van is rigged. As soon as you took the road out of the city, we started following you. What are you doing here?"

He'd never tell them. He wouldn't tell them a thing.

"This is not right. And I wish I could show you why. I wish I could show you what life feels like without that damn Siero messing up your brain."

John didn't even flinch. His arms were steady as he pointed the gun to Winston's chest. The men around him stood waiting, all guns pointing at him, too. The water tank was just behind him, a huge cement pool that he could access through a ladder on the side. Even if he ran as fast as he could, he would never make it to the top. He would never be able to drop the vial inside.

But it was okay. Everything would be okay.

Winston looked up to the ceiling, wishing that he could see the sky, instead.

"I'm sorry, Anna. I have to break my promise."

Before he could change his mind, Winston turned to the side and raced to the metallic ladder.

Gunshots resounded in the enclosed space, like explosions being detonated right inside his head. He fell against the ladder, his fingers barely brushing the first step, and the vial falling to the ground with a clinking sound that no one heard. His back burned as if a thousand whips had scorched his skin, and his breathing came out ragged as he struggled to hold onto his life — even if just for a second longer. Even if just to remember what Anna's smile looked like.

Before everything went dark, Winston managed to smile as his left hand felt the empty vial in his pocket. He had been a fool, but the Military had been too slow. The second vial had been the decoy, and the first had already been emptied into the tank that contained the chemicals used to purify the water.

He'd broken his promise to live for the both of them, but at least, they'd be reunited soon.

EPILOGUE

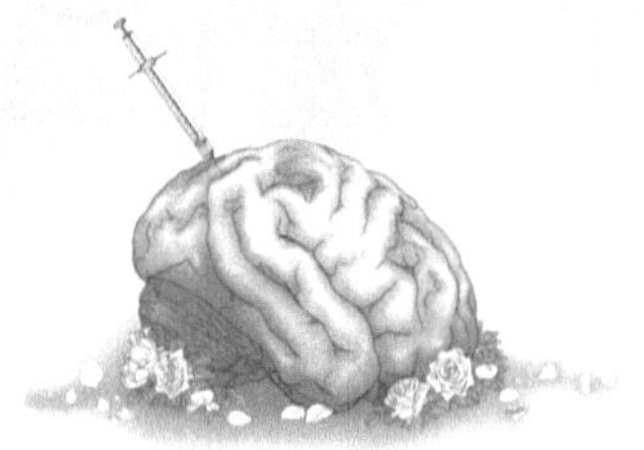

FAULKNER

The town of Bellevue was a messed-up place. The working class was outside Faulkner's building, and he knew it wouldn't be long until they found their way into his office. It was a raging war outside, and Faulkner hid for as long as he could, making desperate calls to try and save his city. A city that was messed up because everyone's emotions had returned in full, and many had lost their minds to it.

Anna Chaplin had come up with a serum right under his nose, one to return emotions to the entire population. And with the help of soldier Hitcher, she had managed to leak her formula into the water supply of the entire town.

Within less than twenty-four hours, people had regained their emotions. Within two days, riots had started. Within three, his own Military had turned against him. Almost forty years had passed since Dr. Faulkner had become the supreme leader of the town of Bellevue, his name had been plastered all over the city, his superiors had praised him, and the government had allowed him to run the town as he pleased as an experiment. And now, no one was returning his calls.

He had the second sample of the antidote that they had retrieved from soldier Hitcher after his demise, and he was pretty sure the results of the revolts were due to a dose too high. The formula had been so concentrated that, when mixed with the chemicals in the purification tanks, it had backfired. The town had lived without emotions their whole lives, and with everything coming back in full so quickly, they had lost their minds, The few who had been used to the emotions vials still regained some of their sanity and had stayed by Faulkner's side longer, but they were all angry at him, regardless. They all wanted him to be taken down.

When the phone finally rang, he picked it up in a blink. He was desperate.

"Faulkner, here, what's taking so long? Why is help not on the way already?"

"Dr. Faulkner, we allowed you to run this town under the premise that the rest of the world wouldn't hear about it. You claimed to have everything under control, and your soldiers helped the nation with wars on multiple occasions. But now, with the Military turning against you and the town completely out of control, we have no choice but to let you loose."

"Let me loose?" Faulkner paled as he slumped in his chair. He could hear the people getting closer. The devoted army at the front of his building had probably fallen. They were coming for him. They were coming to eradicate him for what he had done. For trying to help them. "You're fools! Fools! I have done everything and more for this town. I have provided valuable assets to the Military. I have done everything, all for my country! For this nation! I demand that you send a helicopter to my roof and retrieve me right now!"

A loud bang sounded below him, and Faulkner hung up. He clutched his phone to his chest and moved as fast as he could toward the elevator. The roof was only on the next floor, but the stairs weren't an option for a man who could barely walk.

He reached the rooftop, panting, his leg throbbing with pain. He looked to the sky, expecting his rescue helicopter. They wouldn't be so stupid as to leave him there. He was a valuable asset to the government. They needed him.

Engines roared in the distance, and Faulkner smiled despite it all.

They did come for me.

But it wasn't a helicopter that showed up between the clouds — it was a plane. Several planes.

Military ones.

Faulkner fell to his knees as he watched in horror, as the plane's hatches opened up, and the bombs were dropped, wiping away the entire city.

EMOTIONAL DEVIANTS

VIOLA TEMPEST